S0-AYP-478

Jackie Lugg's Book
Lena Waters
Sharon Lee Pleas

THE SECRET IN THE
OLD ATTIC

"SO SHE FOUND IT FOR ME!" HE GLOATED.

The Secret in the Old Attic

NANCY DREW MYSTERY STORIES

THE SECRET IN THE OLD ATTIC

BY

CAROLYN KEENE

ILLUSTRATED BY

RUSSELL H. TANDY

NEW YORK

GROSSET & DUNLAP

PUBLISHERS

Made in the United States of America

CONTENTS

THE SECRET IN THE
OLD ATTIC

CHAPTER 1

A Challenge

"This seems like a strange place to hunt for a clue, Nancy, but that is exactly what I've been asked to do."

The girl's father, Carson Drew, a lawyer, gazed at a package of letters tied with blue ribbon, which he had taken from his pocket and laid on the dinner table.

"What is the clue about?" asked Nancy, watching eagerly as he tried to untie the ribbon.

"Some lost music."

"Music? What kind?"

"Popular songs, I believe, which haven't been published yet," replied Mr. Drew. "This task isn't exactly to my liking. I understand these are love letters, and——"

Nancy laughed. Her father was the outstanding attorney of River Heights, and had won many difficult cases by his brilliant, clear thinking. It was humorous to see him working industriously at a ribbon knot to untie a bundle of love letters! The girl offered to do it for him, and he looked relieved.

"Please tell me more about the case," Nancy begged. "Maybe I can help you with it."

1

"I believe you can," replied her father with a smile.

He looked affectionately at the slim, blue-eyed girl beside him. Mr. Drew was proud of his attractive and unusually talented daughter, who had gained a reputation of her own by solving several mysteries. She and her father had been very close since the death of Mrs. Drew a number of years before, and had come to depend on each other for advice and assistance in their problems.

Mr. Drew realized that some day Nancy probably would marry and leave him, but he hoped that this would not happen for a long time. She had many friends, both boys and girls. Her special chums were Bess Marvin and Bess's cousin, a girl named George Fayne. The boy who seemed to interest Nancy most, her father had noticed, was Ned Nickerson, now a student at Emerson College.

"Dad, if you don't want to take the case of the missing music," Nancy said, her eyes sparkling, "then I'll be glad to. Tell me what to look for in these letters."

"I don't know," her father replied. "The instructions were vague. This afternoon, while I was away from my office, an elderly man named Philip March called and left this package with my secretary. He asked that I look through the letters to see if there is any hint as to what might have become of certain songs."

"Who composed them?" asked Nancy.

"I don't know."

Nancy had untied the ribbon, and now handed the letters to her father. He pulled one from its envelope and read it hastily.

"I don't find any clue here," the lawyer said a few moments later. "Read this, Nancy, and see what you make of it."

His daughter eagerly scanned the letter. It had been written by a soldier named Fipp to his wife Connie four years before.

"I don't see any clue either," Nancy said. "Do you suppose Fipp is a nickname for Philip, and he's Mr. March's son?"

"Probably," agreed Mr. Drew, handing the other letters to his daughter. "I'm mighty embarrassed reading these. Love letters never were meant to be read by the outside world."

Nancy respected her father's opinion. Yet she felt that if Mr. March were a close relative of the writer, he would not have shown the letters to anyone unless he had good reason for doing so.

"Have you ever met Mr. March?" she asked.

"1 think not. But he may be a member of a family that lived on an estate up the river a few miles. It seems to me there is an interesting story connected with them, but I can't recall what it is. Well, we'll soon know about the letters. Mr. March is coming here this evening."

Nancy was eager for the moment to arrive

when the man would ring the doorbell. While she waited, she re-read the letters, pausing at several lovely verses in them. Nowhere, however, could she find any clue to lost or hidden music.

"Do you suppose these verses are the words of the songs?" she mused. "Maybe they're——"

Just then the doorbell rang and Nancy hurried to admit the caller. He was an elderly, gray-haired gentleman of soldierly bearing. His clothes were somewhat worn, but his shoes were polished and his suit neatly pressed. He bowed politely to Nancy and introduced himself as Philip March.

"Oh, yes, my father is expecting you. Please come in," the girl invited.

Nancy led the man into the living room where Carson Drew was waiting. When she started to leave, Mr. March invited her to stay and hear his story. He sank wearily into a chair.

"I owe you an apology, Mr. Drew, for asking such a strange favor," he began in a tired voice. "A feeling of desperation came over me this afternoon. On the spur of the moment I decided to come to your office. You and your daughter have helped so many people, I thought you might give me some advice."

Mr. March was very pale and ill-at-ease. To give him time to compose himself, Nancy offered to bring him a glass of water. This seemed to refresh him somewhat and Mr. Drew then inquired kindly if the writer of the letters was someone close to him.

"Yes, he was my son. My only son," the caller said sadly. "In fact, he was my only child. Like myself, he was a soldier, but he lost his life four years ago fighting in a foreign land."

"I'm sorry to hear that," said Mr. Drew sympathetically, and Nancy added a word of condolence.

"Fipp—that's what my Philip called himself when he was a little boy, and the name stuck," Mr. March went on. "Fipp was married to a lovely girl, but she passed away soon after he did. Now all I have is little Susan."

"She is your grandchild?" asked Nancy.

"Yes. Susan is six years old, and I want to keep her with me, but—" The old man closed his eyes as if to shut out an unpleasant picture. "I face complete poverty and will lose Susan and my home, unless Fipp's music can be found and sold."

"Please tell us more about the music," begged Nancy, touched by the man's story.

"Perhaps I should start by telling you of my family. The Marches have been proud, well-to-do people—several generations of us in River Heights. I'm not going to be the one to ask for charity. Fipp wouldn't want me to."

As Mr. March paused to take another drink of water, Carson Drew inquired how the lost music could bring him any money.

"The songs were never published," the caller replied. "And they were very fine." He turned to Nancy. "The kind of up-to-date music you young people like, but much better than a lot of it I hear."

Nancy was interested at once.

"My son could not bring himself to take the songs to a publisher, for he was never quite satisfied with his work," Mr. March explained. "Then, just before he became a soldier, Fipp put the music away in some secret place. If it can only be found and sold, little Susan will be taken care of until she is grown up."

"Mr. March, what made you think there is a clue to the songs in these letters?" asked Nancy, already thinking of how she could help the little girl and her grandfather.

"Connie, Susan's mother, wrote to Fipp, suggesting that he tell us where the music was. The boy was full of fun, and replied that he'd give her a hint and she could look for it. Then, after a few more letters"—at this point the old man bowed his head—"no others came."

There followed several moments of silence; then Mr. Drew spoke. "Mr. March, my daughter and I could not find a clue, but perhaps we can if we study the letters more thoroughly."

"Thank you, thank you," the elderly soldier murmured. "I'll remember your kindness always. I'd never ask your help for myself— only for Susan. Friends have been caring for her lately, but they're moving away and are bringing her back to me the first of the week. I must do something very soon. Otherwise, Susan will be lost to me.''

Mr. March rose stiffly to his feet. He bowed to Nancy, shook hands with Mr. Drew, and started slowly toward the door. Midway across the room, he swayed slightly and grasped a corner of the piano for support.

"Mr. March! You're ill!" Nancy cried, darting to his side.

As she seized the man's arm, he slumped and collapsed in a faint onto a couch. When Nancy and her father failed to revive him, the girl ran for Hannah Gruen, their housekeeper. She could not restore Mr. March to consciousness, either, so Mr. Drew called in Doctor Evans.

"How serious is it?" the lawyer asked him, as soon as the examination was over. "A heart attack?"

"Fortunately, no," replied the doctor. "The man is simply undernourished. What he needs is a few days' complete rest and plenty of good, wholesome food."

"Let's keep him here, Dad," Nancy begged.

Her father approved heartily, and he and the doctor carried the patient upstairs to the guest room. While Doctor Evans administered to him, Nancy and the housekeeper hurried to the kitchen to prepare food.

"I'll fix a bowl of broth," said Mrs. Gruen, bustling about. "Make some toast, Nancy," she directed.

Everyone in the house was so busy waiting on Mr. March that they failed to notice a uniformed messenger boy who came up the steps of the front porch. Furthermore, they did not see a girl who hastened across the street and spoke to the boy before he had a chance to ring the doorbell.

After making sure that the telegram he was about to deliver was for Nancy Drew, the mysterious stranger signed for it, tipped the boy, and pretended to enter the house. What she actually did was to wait on the porch until the messenger had disappeared down the street. Then she tiptoed away, tore open the sealed envelope, and read the communication by the light of a street lamp.

"I'll answer this myself," she smiled, a self-satisfied look on her face, and hastened away.

CHAPTER II

THE OLD HOUSE

UNAWARE that she was to have received an important message, Nancy helped Mrs. Gruen make Mr. March as comfortable as possible. They were relieved that he had regained consciousness and was eating the food they offered him.

"Now if you'll help me to the bus," he said when he had finished, "I'll trouble you no longer."

"Indeed, you'll not stir from that bed!" the kind-hearted housekeeper replied firmly. "You are to remain here until you feel strong."

Too weak to protest, Mr. March submitted, stating he would leave in the morning. But when morning came, Nancy persuaded him to stay by telling him she needed more information about the missing music.

"You take it easy today, and tomorrow we'll go over the letters together," she coaxed him.

During the day Nancy brought up trays of food to the elderly soldier and encouraged him to talk about himself. She found him to be a delightful, cultured person, who had fought in the first World War. The past few years he had not been strong and therefore had been unable to work very much.

"I want you to see my house sometime," he said late that afternoon. "Of course, it doesn't look like it used to—I don't make a very good housekeeper, and I haven't been able to afford one, or a gardener either, for a long time."

"How old is the house?" asked Nancy.

"Over two hundred years; at least, part of it is. Fact of the matter is, the first Marches had slaves. The slave quarters are still there."

"How intriguing!" exclaimed Nancy. "When you're well enough to go home, I'll drive you there and you can show the place to me."

In the midst of this conversation, the doorbell rang. Nancy excused herself and hurried below. Hannah Gruen, who had answered the summons, was now admitting two girls.

"Hi, Nancy!" said one of the callers. "What do you know?"

Nancy greeted them with a smile.

"My goodness, George Fayne!" she exclaimed, looking at her friend's head. "If you have much more hair cut off, people will really think you're a boy."

"Suits me," giggled the slender brunette. She went to the living room radio and turned it on to a program of dance music. "Buck Rodman must like my hair this way, or he wouldn't have asked me to the dance."

"Nancy, we came to find out if you're going to get a new dress for the big affair," said Bess

Marvin, the pretty, slightly plump girl with George.

"Please tell me what you're talking about," begged Nancy.

"Full of mystery as usual," laughed Bess. "You know well enough we mean the dance at Emerson College, and we know you're going with Ned Nickerson, but we don't know what you plan to wear."

"You're teasing me," Nancy accused.

Bess and George pretended to look hurt. "Why so secretive?" asked George.

"Girls, I know nothing about the dance, and I've not been invited," declared Nancy.

"Not been invited!" exploded the other two.

They decided that Ned must have been very busy and had not had time to get in touch with Nancy.

"But he will any minute," Bess prophesied. Just then the telephone rang. "There he is now, I'll bet," she added.

Nancy went quickly to the telephone in the hall. The call was for her, but it was not from Ned Nickerson. It was from another young man by the name of Horace Lally, a senior at Emerson College. He was an attractive-looking youth, but very conceited. Nancy did not like him. To her dismay, he invited her to the dance.

"Oh, I don't believe I can go," she answered, sparring for time. "Thanks a lot, just the same."

"I won't take 'No' for an answer," Horace insisted. "I'll call you again tomorrow."

He hung up before the girl had a chance to protest. None too happy, Nancy returned to tell her friends about the conversation.

"Why not go with Horace just to tease Ned?" suggested Bess. "It would serve him right for being so slow in asking you."

Nancy shook her head. "If Ned should invite me, I'd accept, of course. But if he shouldn't, I'd certainly not go with Horace just to get there."

Skillfully she changed the subject by saying she had a new mystery to solve and telling George and Bess about Mr. March. The girls were interested, but kept coming back to the topic of the dance. Nancy felt slightly relieved when they left the house. Alone once more, she sat down in a chair near the radio to think.

"I wonder if Ned will call me," she mused.

The broadcast was still on, a trumpet playing a haunting melody with orchestral accompaniment. Nancy was so deep in thought that she paid no attention to it.

"Maybe Ned has asked another girl," she meditated. "He has a perfect right to, of course."

She arose, turned off the radio, and went into the hall. As she walked up the stairs, she was startled by an excited cry from Mr. March. She took the steps two at a time and ran into his room.

"That melody!" the old soldier shouted. "It was my son's!"

"You mean the one you heard on the radio?"

"Yes. He never had it published! The song has been stolen! You must find the thief!" the man cried, fairly beside himself.

Upon several occasions Nancy had been asked to locate thieves of one kind or another. Since the time she had solved the mystery known as The Secret of the Old Clock, she had enjoyed a rather enviable reputation as an amateur detective. Only recently she had shown up a schemer in a case called The Clue in the Jewel Box, saving a fortune for the unusual Madame Alexandra. But to locate a plagiarist who had stolen songs and published them as his own was an assignment quite different from anything she had ever attempted.

"I'll do all I can to help you," Nancy promised Mr. March, hurrying to the radio in her own bedroom.

She turned it on, but the program of dance music was over. She did not even know which station it had come from, and a list she looked up in the newspaper was not very helpful. Three similar programs had been on at the same time!

"I suppose I could write to all the stations for a list of selections the bands played today," Nancy reflected, "but maybe I won't have to. The tune Mr. March says is his son's surely will be played again."

She decided to take her radio into the guest room so the elderly man could listen for the song. He listened attentively all day, but up to the time he was ready to go to sleep that evening, the elderly man had not heard the special melody again. He insisted still that it was a composition of his son's.

"Fipp was very talented," he declared proudly, as Nancy smoothed the bed sheets and turned his pillow. "Why, my son could play six different instruments. When he lived at home, he would lock himself in the attic and compose for hours at a time. Then when the pieces were finished, he would come downstairs to the music room and play them for the family."

"Do you know of anyone who might have stolen your son's work?" Nancy asked thoughtfully.

Mr. March shook his head. "Nobody," he replied.

The girl realized that she would have to proceed cautiously in any investigation. She could not accuse a person of plagiarism until she had some proof. Her task now was twofold: locate the thief and trace the rest of the unpublished music. She and Mr. March read Fipp's letters again, but as before Nancy could find no clue in any of them.

"Mr. March," she said slowly, "I suppose you've searched the music room and the rest of your home for your son's songs?"

"Oh, many times. But to no purpose."

"How about the attic?"

"I've looked there, too," the man replied. "But it was no use. The songs are missing, and it's my belief now, after hearing the one over the radio, that maybe all of them have been stolen."

The next day when the doctor pronounced Mr. March strong enough to go home, Nancy said she would take him there in her car. She invited Bess and George to accompany them.

"I'm sorry to have you see my estate so run down," the elderly soldier said as they rode along. "There was a time when it was one of the show places of River Heights."

The afternoon was gloomy. As the car approached the river, dark clouds scudded across the sky.

"There's the house—yonder through that pine grove," Mr. March directed presently. "It's called Pleasant Hedges."

The name hardly suited the estate, for the hedges were untrimmed and interspersed with weeds. Long blades of grass covered the lawn. Several old pine trees stood near the house. The wind whispered dismally through the swaying boughs.

"It's almost spooky," Bess said in a hushed voice to Nancy on the front seat.

The house was a rambling structure, partly covered with vines. There was a stone section at one end, but the rest was built of clapboards, now badly weatherbeaten. A loose shutter swung back and forth, creaking on its rusty hinges.

"Now that we're here, may we look inside the house, Mr. March?" Nancy asked as she drew up at the front door. "It's possible the four of us together might find that lost music."

"I'll be grateful if you'll try," replied the owner. "Your young eyes no doubt are sharper than mine."

As Nancy gazed at the stone wing, she thought that it appeared to be much older than the rest of the house and asked Mr. March about it.

"That part was built way back when people around here had slaves," he explained. "I'll show you that first."

He led his callers along a weed-grown path to some moss-covered steps.

"The lower level of the old building was a stable," the elderly man explained.

The girls descended the steps and looked inside the strange place. It was dirty and cobwebby from years of disuse. The long rows of empty stalls, each with a name posted above it, fascinated them.

"*Running Mate*," Bess read aloud. "And here's another—*Kentucky Blue*. How interesting!"

"Those were the names of two of my grandfather's horses," Mr. March explained. "Great racers they were in their day. The Marches kept a stable which was known throughout the country. The jockeys lived upstairs in the former slave quarters.''

He pointed to a narrow stairway. The girls climbed up and looked into the little rooms which ran off a center hallway.

"What a story this place could tell," sighed Bess. "Old mammies crooning, little pickaninnies dancing——"

"You certainly have a good imagination," said George practically. "Without a piece of furniture or a rug or a picture in the place, how can you think of such things?"

Nancy had been looking around carefully for any possible hiding places in the walls or floors where Fipp March might have put away the music he had composed. She did not see one anywhere.

"Use your imagination, Bess, to find the missing songs," she laughed.

"No, thanks. Too—too many mice," the girl cried, as one scurried across the floor at that very moment.

The three girls descended the antique stairway, which groaned beneath their weight. Mr. March escorted them back to the main entrance of the house. From his pocket he took a large brass key. After several attempts he succeeded in unlocking the heavy Colonial door, and it swung open with a grating sound.

"The place is pretty bare," the owner said with a sigh. "I've sold nearly all the good furniture. Had to do it to raise money for little Susan."

The girls walked into the long, empty hall, which sent out hollow echoes when they spoke. From there Mr. March led them to the music room. The only furniture it held was an old-fashioned piano with yellowed keys and a threadbare chair in front of it.

Several other rooms on the first floor were empty and dismal. Heavy silken draperies, once beautiful, but now faded and torn, hung at some of the windows. The dining room still had its walnut table, chairs, and buffet, but a built-in corner cupboard was bare.

"I sold the fine old glass and china that used to be in there," Mr. March said to Nancy in a strained voice. "It seemed best. Come, we'll go upstairs now."

Three of the bedrooms on the second floor were furnished, but they did not contain the lovely old mahogany or walnut bedsteads and bureaus one might have expected. Inexpensive modern pieces had taken the place of those which had been sold.

Realizing how desperately Mr. March needed money, Nancy kept her eyes open for any objects that might be taken to antique dealers. Apparently almost everything of value had been removed already. She asked if the girls might search for the missing music.

"Go right ahead," Mr. March told her.

For an hour she, Bess, and George tapped

walls, looked into cupboards beside the fire-
places, and examined every inch of floor for re-
movable boards. Three times Nancy inspected
the pine-paneled music room. There seemed to
be no clue anywhere.

"Nothing is left now but the attic," said the
young detective to Mr. March at last. "May
we go up there?"

"I'll show you the way. It's a long, steep
climb," he declared, unlocking the door to a
stairway. "I don't go up here very often. It
winds me."

Pausing frequently to catch his breath, the
elderly man conducted the girls up the dark
steps.

"I should have brought a candle," he apologized. "There are no lights up here, but
maybe you can see well enough by the light
from the window."

As he reached the top step, they suddenly
heard a loud pounding noise from somewhere
downstairs.

"What was that?" Bess asked, startled.

They all listened intently.

"It sounded to me as if someone might be
hammering on a door!" declared George.

Nancy offered to run below to find out, but
Mr. March would not hear of this.

"No, I'll go," he insisted. "You girls might
search the attic in the meantime."

Left to themselves, Nancy, George, and Bess
scrambled into the attic. It was so dark that at

first they could see nothing. As soon as Nancy's eyes became accustomed to the dimness, she groped her way to the window, grimy with dirt, and opened it.

At the same moment Bess gave a little shriek. A thick, dust-laden cobweb had brushed against her mouth.

"This place is horrible!" she said with distaste. "Worse than the slave quarters."

A mahogany cane lay across an old trunk. Snatching it up, the girl prodded several of the flimsy cobwebs, winding them round and round the stick.

"The attic is really very interesting," Nancy said, surveying the assortment of boxes and trunks. She called her friends' attention to a fine old table which stood in a corner. "I believe Mr. March could sell that!" she cried enthusiastically. "And look at these old-fashioned bandboxes!"

She picked up one of the round, cardboard hatboxes. On it was the picture of a gay rural scene of early American life.

"Let me see that!" exclaimed Bess, blowing off the dust. "Why, Mr. March could get something for this. Only yesterday Mother told me about a bandbox like this which brought a good price at an auction sale."

"There are at least a dozen of them here!" George declared. "All in good condition, too."

They were decorated with pictures of eagles, flowers, and various scenes of American history.

Two of them contained velvet bonnets with feather ornaments.

"Girls, this attic may be a valuable find!" Nancy said excitedly.

"Even if we don't locate the missing music, there may be other things here Mr. March can sell," added George. "Let's look."

Bess was not paying attention, for a bat had just flown through the open window. The blind little creature was coming directly toward her!

"Oh! Oh!" she gasped, ducking her head. "Look out, girls!"

At this moment there came an agonized cry from below. It was followed by a shout.

Rushing to the stairway, Nancy listened anxiously. She heard Mr. March calling her name in a distressed tone.

"Come quickly! I need your help!" the elderly man was crying.

CHAPTER III

A Lost Child

THOROUGHLY alarmed, Nancy and her friends at once abandoned their search of the attic, hurrying down the steep stairway as fast as they could.

"What can be wrong?" Bess gasped.

"Maybe Mr. March has fallen and hurt himself," declared Nancy uneasily.

The girls could not locate the elderly soldier anywhere on the second floor. Descending to the first, they were relieved to find him uninjured. He was talking excitedly to a strange woman.

"This is Mrs. French. She has been looking after Susan," he explained quickly. "She brings me dreadful news. My little granddaughter is missing!"

"Missing!" the girls echoed.

"It's not my fault," Mrs. French spoke up quickly. "I've been caring for Susan as I would my own daughter. But yesterday, while she was playing in the garden, she disappeared."

"Maybe she ran away," said George bluntly. "My little cousin did."

22

"I don't know why she should have. Susan seemed to be very happy with me," replied Mrs. French. "I have no idea what has become of her. We've searched the neighborhood."

"No one saw her leave the garden?" asked Nancy.

"Not a soul. Oh, I feel sick about it. This morning I thought maybe she had tried to find her way back here. Now I hear you haven't seen her."

"If Susan came here yesterday, she wouldn't have found me. And she wouldn't have known what to do," said Mr. March. "Oh, we must hunt for her right away!"

"The first thing to do is notify the police," suggested Nancy. "Or has that already been done?"

"I called them immediately," Mrs. French told her. "They haven't a single clue yet."

The woman collapsed into a chair, sobbing. Nancy sought to comfort both her and Mr. March, while she tried to figure out what could be done. It was possible that little Susan had been kidnaped, though it seemed more likely that the child was lost.

"Susan is too small to look after herself," Mr. March said brokenly. "Last night it rained, too. If she's lost in the woods——"

"Please try not to think of that," Nancy begged him. "We'll find Susan."

It had occurred to her that she might summon the members of a hiking club to which she belonged and organize a searching party. Everyone in the group was familiar with the territory. By going over it in an ever-narrowing circle, they surely would find the little girl.

"I'll telephone some of my friends. They'll help us!" Nancy encouraged Mr. March. "And so will my father."

The old mansion had no telephone, so Nancy drove quickly to the nearest neighbor to put in the calls. As the alarm spread, dozens of men and women, young and middle-aged, came to assist. Mr. Drew directed the older group, Nancy the hiking club.

Throughout the afternoon the hunt continued. Darkness came on, and with it deep discouragement. Little Susan had not been found, though many miles of countryside had been combed.

"Nancy, you're nearly exhausted," her father protested at last. "You must go home and rest. I'll carry on here."

The girl shook her head. "I can't go until Susan is found, Dad."

The March place had been made the headquarters for the searching parties. Group after group came back to report failure, and many gave up. Nancy's hiking club friends remained faithful, however, long after the others had gone home.

"It's just no use," Bess declared, as the night wore on. She, Nancy, and George were standing in front of the house. "Susan is not going to be found. I'm sure she was kidnaped. Why not go home and get some sleep, Nancy?"

"No, I want to stay here."

"We've sure hunted everywhere," George added wearily. "If I could think of another place, I'd look there, but we've covered every inch of ground for miles around."

Across the river they could see the bobbing flashlights of the last searching party. A cool wind penetrated the light clothing the girls wore.

"I hate to think of poor little Susan out-of-doors on such a chilly night," Bess commented. "She may be in a dreadful state when she is found."

Nancy had seated herself on the porch steps, a faraway look in her eyes. If the child had not been kidnaped and was not lost in the neighborhood, what could have become of her? After a few moments the girl got up suddenly, saying she wanted to search the barn.

"It's the only place we haven't looked," she said.

George and Bess followed, but both thought the move useless.

"The barn's locked," protested George. "Anyway, if Susan is in there, she'd have made a noise long ago and we'd have heard her."

"Unless something happened to her in there," said Nancy, worried. "She might have come here, found the house locked, and gone into the barn to get out of the rain last night. The door may have slammed shut, and——"

Nancy's reasoning made Bess tremble. She almost dreaded finding Susan now, for she feared the worst. In that event, how could they ever break the bad news to Mr. March?

The barn door was not locked, but it was so heavy that it took the combined strength of the three girls to pull it open. Nancy stopped short on the threshold.

"What was that?" she asked in a low voice.

"I didn't hear anything," murmured George.

"Neither did I," said Bess.

Nancy waved her flashlight about. All was still now.

The girls stepped inside the building. Immediately a gust of wind slammed the door shut behind them. Bess jumped.

"I don't like this place," she said with a shiver.

As she spoke, the girls heard a wailing sound which seemed to come from the hayloft.

"There *is* someone in here!" Nancy exclaimed. "I'm going to climb up into the loft and look around."

"Let's call one of the men," Bess urged nervously. "You don't know what you'll find."

Nancy would not wait. Rapidly she mounted the ladder. A moment later the two girls below heard her shout joyously.

"I've found Susan! Come on up!"

Bess and George climbed the ladder as fast as they could. They found Nancy kneeling beside a disheveled child huddled in the hay.

"I've found her!" Nancy declared excitedly. "But she's ill!"

The little girl, her face red with fever, cringed away from her rescuers in fear. Blinded by the flashlight, she buried her head in the mound of hay.

"Don't be afraid," Nancy soothed her. "We've come to take you to your grandfather. You're Susan March, aren't you?"

The words "grandfather" and "March" seemed to bring the child out of her frightened state. She began to sob as if her heart would break.

"Granapa went off and left me," she wailed. "He locked the door so I couldn't get in. Why did my grandpa go away?"

"Your grandfather has been ill," Nancy explained kindly. "He's home now, though, and has been trying to find you. Come, we'll take you to him."

She helped the child to her feet, brushing hay from the crumpled gingham dress.

"I don't feel good," Susan confessed as they half carried her to the ladder.

"You'll soon be in your own bed. Then you'll feel better," Nancy said comfortingly. "Why did you leave Mrs. French?" she asked.

"Some gypsies came along the street and I followed them," Susan explained. "Then I couldn't find Mrs. French's house. So I came to grandpa's. But he wasn't here."

"So you decided to sleep in the barn?" prompted Nancy, lifting the child down the ladder.

"No. A bad man came to the house. He walked so quiet I was afraid of him, so I ran to the barn."

"And hid in the hay?"

"Yes. The big door banged shut and I couldn't open it. I got sick so I went back to the hay and went to sleep."

"Poor child," said Bess, tears coming to her eyes.

Nancy wondered who the "bad man" might have been. She thought it best not to question the little girl further just then. She was too frightened and ill.

"My eyes hurt," the child added wistfully, "and I'm awful hot."

This gave Nancy an idea. When they reached the floor of the barn, she turned the beam of her flashlight full on Susan's chest.

"Measles, I guess," she announced, noting the red blotches. "That's a shame."

"As if poor Mr. March hasn't enough trouble without this!" whispered Bess to George. "What will he do?"

"I'm never going to leave my grandfather again," Susan said pitifully. "He loves me more than anyone in the world."

"Mr. March hasn't enough money to send his granddaughter to the hospital," thought Nancy. "And Mrs. French shouldn't take her back." Aloud she said, "Girls, do you remember Effie?"

"That dizzy maid who works for your family once in a while?" laughed George. "How could one forget her?"

"Effie isn't exactly dizzy," Nancy corrected. "She can be very efficient, as long as she isn't involved in a mystery. I believe I'll see if she can come here."

"This old homestead already has the makings of a mystery," thought George significantly.

"Effie would be the solution to the housekeeping problem," Nancy went on. "I hope Mr. March will agree to having her here."

The girls carried little Susan into the house and placed her in her own bed. Mr. March wept in relief.

"My little pet!" he said, caressing the child tenderly. "Never go away again, Susan, my dear."

"No, never, never," the little girl promised.

"I'm so happy that she is safe," the elderly man murmured to Nancy and her friends, "that nothing else matters. Oh, I do thank you from the bottom of my heart for finding her."

He was so delighted to see his granddaughter that it was some time before he realized she was ill. Finally Nancy told him what the trouble probably was.

"I'm so glad it's nothing worse," he said. Then suddenly he remembered that he was almost penniless. "But what am I to do? I've never taken care of a sick child. Susan has always been so well."

This was Nancy's opportunity to mention Effie as a possible housekeeper. The problem of salary worried Grandfather March.

"I have a surprise for you," Nancy smiled.

"Just before you called us from the attic, we found several fine old bandboxes and a table which can be sold. The money from them will take care of things for a while."

The elderly man looked at the girl gratefully. "You have been so good," he said. "I guess some kind Providence led me to your door to ask your help for little Susan."

"As soon as things get straightened out here, I'll go on searching for the music," promised Nancy. "I haven't forgotten about it."

While she tried to make Susan comfortable with the meager supplies in the house, Bess and George went off to notify Mr. Drew and the other searchers that the child had been found. When morning came, Bess became nurse, and Nancy drove off to telephone to Doctor Evans and go to Effie's house.

The maid, kind-hearted and loyal to the Drew family, easily was persuaded to take charge at Pleasant Hedges. However, when first she glimpsed the huge, barren old dwelling, she almost changed her mind.

"Oh! Oh!" she wailed. "What am I gettin' into? Another mystery? This old place looks haunted to me! I believe I'd better go home!"

Nancy finally persuaded the girl to stay. As she began her work, the maid forgot her fears. Nancy had bought some food, and soon Effie was starting a hot breakfast.

"I've done all I can for the time being," Nancy said wearily to Mr. March, declining his invitation to stay to eat. "I'm going home to get some sleep."

"You more than deserve it," he replied. "I never can thank you and your friends enough for what you have done for me," and his voice trembled with feeling as he spoke.

The girls put the table and bandboxes in the car and drove away. Nancy dropped Bess and George off at their homes. Then she went on to the Drew residence.

Her father had just finished his breakfast and was about to read his morning mail. A number of letters lay on the table.

"Anything for me?" Nancy asked as soon as she had kissed her father and told him what had happened at the March home after he had left.

He handed her an envelope. Nancy's pulse stepped up a bit, for she read "Emerson College" in the left-hand corner. Had Ned—? Then her spirits fell as she noted the name of the sender—Horace Lally.

"Aren't you going to read your letter?" Mr. Drew inquired as Nancy laid aside the envelope.

"I can guess what it says. Horace wants an answer to his invitation to the dance."

"Will you go?"

"Not with him."

With a sigh, Nancy slit open the envelope and read the message. As she had expected, Horace urgently asked her to be his guest. He ended the letter with:

"If you do not attend the affair, you'll always regret it. There's to be a special surprise announcement which you can't afford to miss."

The invitation disturbed Nancy. She was not willing to go with Horace under any circumstances, but she kept wondering what the important surprise he had mentioned in his letter might be. Moreover, should Ned Nickerson ask her now, she felt that it would hardly be proper for her to accept.

"Why be foolish, Nancy?" Bess argued, dropping in with George late that afternoon. "Surely you could forget Ned and endure Horace for one evening! We want you to go."

"If you don't want to go with him, then come along with Bess and me," added George persuasively. "We'll find a date for you and show Ned a thing or two!"

Nancy refused to be coaxed by her friends, although she promised to wait until the next day before replying to Horace's letter. By morning she had not changed her mind, however, and wrote her regrets to the young man.

"Surprise or no surprise, I can't go with him!" she told herself. "Bess and George will have to hear the announcement and tell me about it."

She had just finished the letter when Hannah Gruen called up the stairway to say that Effie was on the telephone.

"Effie!" exclaimed Nancy, dropping her pen. "I hope nothing is wrong."

Nancy dashed down the steps two at a time to reach the telephone in the lower hall. At first the maid talked so fast and in such an excited voice that the Drew girl was unable to distinguish a word she said.

"Effie, calm down! I don't know what you're saying! Has anything happened to Susan?"

"Susan is all right," the maid admitted in a quieter tone.

"Then what is wrong?"

"Everything! Oh, I'm scared! I don't want to stay!"

"Tell me what happened."

"Last night—" Effie paused.

"Yes?" Nancy prompted her.

"I—I—I'm calling from a neighbor's house. I better not tell you any more. Please get out here as fast as you can!"

CHAPTER IV

A SHADOWY FIGURE

NANCY lost no time in driving to the old March homestead. Effie met her at the front door.

"Let's talk outside," the maid whispered. "I don't want Mr. March to hear me. He gets so excited if anything goes wrong."

Nancy hid a smile. This was exactly what Effie herself did. However, she followed the maid to a corner of the lawn.

"Now tell me everything," she urged.

Effie glanced carefully about her. Then in a half-whisper she began her story.

"It happened late last night. I kept hearin' creakin' sounds and couldn't sleep. So I got up. I was standin' lookin' out the bedroom window when all of a sudden I seen a big, powerful-built man sneakin' across the lawn!"

"Had he come from the house?"

"He must have. He came around from the back and stole off toward the barn. Then he disappeared. Oh, I don't like this place! Can't we take little Susan and go into town?"

"We shouldn't move her while she's ill," replied Nancy. "After all, you don't *know* the man was in the house. There isn't anything valuable here for anyone to steal."

"I guess that's right," Effie conceded. "And I saw to it that all the doors and windows were locked before I went to bed."

"Suppose we go around now and see if any of them were forced last night. Which ones did you open this morning?"

"Only the dining room and kitchen."

Together they inspected the first floor of the house. Mr. March was upstairs with Susan, unaware of their investigations. After each window had been checked and found to have been untouched by any intruder, Effie felt somewhat relieved.

"I guess that man wasn't in here after all," she said with a sigh. "But just the same I don't like strange men sneakin' around."

The maid returned to her work, apparently no longer disturbed, for she began to sing. Nancy was far from being undisturbed, however. She went outside again to examine the yard. To her dismay she discovered freshly-made footprints in the soft earth. They circled the house, then led away from a point near the former slave quarters.

"Effie *did* see someone!" she thought. "But what would a prowler be interested in here?"

Again Nancy followed the circle of footsteps around the mansion.

"I don't see how anyone could have entered the house except through a door," she mused.

Then an alarming thought struck her. "Maybe he had a skeleton key!"

Another idea leaped into Nancy's mind. Perhaps the trespasser had been looking for Fipp March's unpublished music! He might even be the one who had stolen the piece Grandfather March had heard on the radio!

Nancy decided to renew her search for the missing compositions at once. On her way to the attic she stopped to say good morning to Susan and Mr. March. The little girl was sitting up in bed, listening to her grandfather tell stories.

"The doctor says I'm almost better, Nancy," the child said happily. "I can get up soon, and I'm never going away from here again—ever!"

Mr. March's eyes glistened with tears, and Nancy was sure she knew what he was thinking. She opened her purse and took out a check made out to the order of Philip March.

"For me? From Mr. Faber's Antique Shop?" the elderly man asked, not understanding.

Nancy nodded. "For your table and bandboxes. The ones my friends and I found in your attic."

"This is unbelievable," said the former soldier. "I had no idea they were worth so much. This will tide me over for several weeks."

"And now I'm going to search for something even more valuable—the music," smiled Nancy.

"I'm sure you won't find it," declared Mr.

March sadly. "I'm afraid it has been stolen."

Nancy did not tell him how near the truth she thought he might be. She said nothing about the prowler of the evening before. Instead, she urged him to be hopeful, and left the room.

She had gone only a few steps when Mr. March started to whistle a lilting tune. Not recognizing the air, Nancy went back and asked him what it was.

"One of the melodies my son composed," the man explained. "This is another which Susan likes."

He hummed a lively tune, and Nancy could not help keeping time with the toe of her shoe.

"Fipp called that *The Gay Bugler,*" the composer's father said proudly.

"It's very catchy," commented Nancy enthusiastically. Then as she listened to one melody after another, she added, "A music publisher would be glad to get them, I'm sure."

"If they're not on the market already," replied Mr. March, shaking his head.

"That's possible, of course, but I've never heard any of them, and I know most of the popular songs that have been published the past few years."

Nancy realized the mystery would be a long way toward being solved if the elderly gentleman could spot some of the tunes on broadcast programs.

"Mr. March, I believe I'll bring my portable

radio out here," she said. "Susan would enjoy listening to it. Besides, you may hear more of your son's songs."

"I'd like that, but won't you need the radio at home?"

"No, we have others. I'll bring the portable tomorrow."

Nancy rearranged the covers on Susan's bed, then started again for the third floor.

"My friends and I didn't have a chance to do much searching in the attic the other day," she told Mr. March. "I guess if the music is any place, it will be there."

"You may be right. But be careful."

When Nancy reached the top of the narrow stairway, she turned on her flashlight and looked about, wondering where to start her hunt. The place seemed even more spooky than the last time she had been there. The floor boards groaned as she stepped forward.

All of a sudden something ahead of her began to move. The girl stared unbelievingly.

A baby's cradle was rocking!

Nancy stole forward. A cold, still feeling came over her. A baby lay asleep in the little bed!

"What in the world is a ba——"

Then she saw that this was not a baby at all, but a large doll. But a doll could not make the cradle rock. Only something alive could do that. Yet there was no one in sight!

"I must have caused a vibration in the floor

that started the rocking," Nancy told herself,
as the cradle suddenly stopped moving. She
wished her heart wouldn't pound so hard and
that she might go on calmly with her work.

In a moment she felt reassured and decided
to begin her search in the old horsehide trunk
standing near her. Nancy fumbled with the
fasteners and tugged at the lid. At first it refused to budge, then it flew open so unexpectedly
that she nearly fell inside. The first thing she
saw was a yellowed wedding gown of rich,
brocaded satin.

"This lovely dress must have belonged to
Susan's grandmother," she thought.

Alongside the gown lay half a dozen old-fashioned pictures. One of them instantly struck
Nancy as familiar.

"I believe this is a Currier and Ives! Yes,
here's the name to prove it!"

Her heart leaped, for she knew how eager
collectors were to buy these old prints.

"What luck this is!" she smiled. "Wonder
what else I can find in here?"

The old trunk yielded a most unusual set of
dishes. They were hand-painted, though not
in conventional designs. Each one had a few
notes of music on it. A fruit basket had several
bars of a melody.

"I must ask Mr. March about this!" Nancy
thought excitedly. "It *might* be a clue."

She decided to go downstairs at once, taking
the bowl with her. Nancy had been so busy

that she had failed to notice a lowering thunder-storm which had been coming nearer and nearer. Now it broke over the old house in all its fury.

"Guess I'd better close the window," she thought, stepping across several boxes to reach it.

After securing it firmly, she went toward the stairs and started down. Just then came a splintering sound, followed by a crash which shook the old March mansion convulsively.

Nancy lost her balance completely. Waving her arms wildly, she pitched forward.

CHAPTER V

Bony Fingers

As Nancy lost her balance on the steep attic stairway, she reached out for the narrow rail at the side, clutching it just in time to save herself from a bad fall. But the fruit bowl crashed to the steps, smashing into a thousand pieces.

Below was pandemonium. Susan was crying loudly, Effie was shrieking, and Mr. March was shouting in an agonized voice:

"Nancy! Nancy Drew, are you all right?"

The girl hurried down and assured him she was unharmed. She in turn was relieved to find the others safe, but Susan was trembling with fright. The little girl had left her bed and had come into the hall. Now she clung piteously to Nancy.

"I don't want to stay alone!" she wailed. "Something fell on the house by my window."

Nancy petted the child and stroked her head soothingly. She asked what had happened. Mr. March, already on his way down the broad staircase to the first floor, replied that he thought one of the big pine trees had blown over and struck the house.

"The—the lightning did it!" declared Effie.

"It—it came down right past the window! I—I—my voice—" She clutched her throat and could not go on.

"Buck up, Effie. The storm's not so bad now," said Nancy. "Let's all of us go downstairs and see what happened."

She got Susan's bathrobe and slippers for her, then together they followed Mr. March. He called to them to come into the music room. Out of a window they could see one of the tall pines leaning against the mansion. As soon as the rain stopped, Nancy and the elderly man went outside to see what damage had been caused.

"Very little harm done," said Mr. March. "This house is well-built. That's a heavy tree. I'm glad it didn't fall on your car."

"I am, too," replied Nancy fervently. "If you'd like me to, I'll go to a garage and get some men to bring a wrecker up here to pull the tree away from the house."

"That would be a good thing to do, but the expense——"

"I know a man who won't charge much," said Nancy. "And that reminds me, I found some more things up in the attic to sell—a dozen or so pictures, a doll, and some dishes. I dropped one, I'm sorry to say."

As she hurried to the attic, Nancy thought how lucky it was that she had not tried to carry all the dishes down before. She opened the window again. Then she gathered up some of the old pieces she had come for. Since there were too many articles for one trip, she decided to take down the big doll and some of the pictures first.

"Susan, I've found something you'll love," she said, handing the silk-dressed "baby" to the little girl.

"Oo," squealed the delighted youngster, "it's bee-autiful, Nancy. Where'd it come from?"

"The attic. Take very good care of the doll. Was it your wife's, Mr. March?"

"Yes," said the child's grandfather. "And she loved it because it was *her* mother's."

"Do you recall the old prints that were stored in the horsehide trunk?" Nancy asked him.

"Oh, those old things?" the soldier replied. "I've meant to burn 'em up, but never got around to it."

"I'm glad you didn't," Nancy laughed. "They'll bring a good price."

"You mean they're worth money?"

"Indeed they are. Mr. Faber will be glad to get them. I've only begun my search of the attic. Let's hope there are many more saleable treasures up there."

"I take it you didn't find any of Fipp's music?"

"Not yet, Mr. March. But I may have found a clue."

Nancy brought down the rest of the pictures and the dishes with the notes of music painted on them.

"Is this a tune your son composed?" she asked hopefully.

She hummed it a couple of times. Mr. March shook his head.

"I don't believe so," he said. "Where did you say you found the dishes? In an old trunk? I've never seen them before."

"Then they didn't belong to your family?"

"I really don't know. Fipp's wife Connie was very handy with the paintbrush. Maybe she painted one of my son's melodies on the bowl."

"In any case, we'd better not sell the dishes," Nancy advised.

As she was about to leave the house, Effie came running toward her.

"Oh, Miss Nancy, you're not going to be away long, are you?" she cried out. "I won't draw a comfortable breath till you return!"

"I'll come back in the morning."

"Morning!" Effie shrieked. "I can't stand it here without you. Creaking sounds, men prowling about at night—Oh, Miss Nancy, please come back and sleep here."

"I'm afraid if it's as bad as you say, I shan't be able to sleep," the Drew girl laughed. "Well, I'll try to get back," she promised as she drove off.

Her first stop was Leonard's Garage. The owner promised to go out to Pleasant Hedges at once and remove the tree. Then Nancy went on to Faber's Shop and received a sizable check for Mr. March. Finally she dropped into her father's office to tell him her plans and also to report what had happened at the March mansion.

"You say Effie saw a man prowling around?" Mr. Drew asked.

"Yes," Nancy replied. "And I found footprints going around the house."

"That's not strange," said her father. "A number of persons were walking about during the search for Susan."

"These prints appear to have been freshly made," Nancy insisted. "And you recall Susan also saw a man. That's why she hid in the barn."

"I don't like that," said Mr. Drew. "If you go back to the mansion, promise me you won't take any chances."

"I promise."

Nancy hugged her father and left his office. She bought a few toys before going home. Later she put them, together with some groceries and her clothes, into a suitcase. With this and the portable radio, she drove back to Pleasant Hedges late in the afternoon.

Unnoticed by her, a dark coupé kept following only a short distance behind. Nancy did not know that it was trailing her. When she turned into the pine grove driveway to the house, the girl driving the coupé stopped and watched her.

"Evidently Nancy Drew is going to stay

here," she muttered to herself. "Oh, I hope she never finds out what I did!"

After Nancy had gone into the old homestead, the other girl tiptoed among the trees and peered at the old mansion. She noticed there was no telephone wire overhead.

"I'm glad of that," she smiled.

Inside the house, Nancy did not hear the mysterious coupé drive away. She had plugged in the portable radio, turning it to a station which was broadcasting a program of popular music.

"By listening to various programs, Mr. March, perhaps you'll hear the song you recognized the other night," she commented. "If you should, please jot down the station, the orchestra, and if it is announced, the name of the composer."

"I'll listen every chance I get," Mr. March promised. "Nothing would please me better than to expose the impostor! I want the world to know Fipp wrote that song!"

The elderly man took the radio upstairs to Susan's room. While Nancy was helping Effie prepare supper, she heard Susan call her.

The girl bounded up the steps. Grandfather March met her at the door of the child's bedroom, a disappointed look on his face.

"We were listening to the radio. I thought I heard Fipp's music, but I was wrong."

While Mr. March was eating his supper downstairs, Nancy remained with Susan. She told the little girl several stories, including one about a certain kind of clever Mother Spider who puts her eggs in a tiny round sac, rolls it along the ground to cover it with dirt, and drops it into a hole.

"None of the spider's enemies notices it, so the babies hatch out without being disturbed," she concluded.

Susan begged for more stories, but Nancy said she had to go downstairs to her own supper. After eating it, she decided to do a little more hunting in the attic. Unfortunately, her flashlight was not working, and she went to the kitchen for a candle.

"I'm certainly glad you're stayin'," said Effie. "This house ain't so bad in the daytime, but when it starts gettin' dark, the shadows just sort of leer at you! The floors have ghosts walkin' on 'em. Hear 'em now!"

"That's only Grandfather March crossing his bedroom," Nancy laughed.

In a cupboard she came upon a long tallow candle. Effie looked at her questioningly.

"There's no light in the attic," explained Nancy, "and I broke my flashlight."

"You're not going up there tonight!" Effie exclaimed, aghast.

"I thought I would," Nancy replied. "There was no chance before supper. I want to look for something."

"Don't go, please. There's no tellin' what danger may be lurkin' up there in the dark!"

"Suppose you come with me."

"Wild horses couldn't drag me up those stairs! Please wait till tomorrow."

"I'm sure nothing will happen to me, Effie, and I want to help Mr. March solve the mystery if I can."

The maid shrugged her shoulders in resignation, as Nancy set the candle in a holder. She left the kitchen, went to the second floor, and stopped at the attic stairway. There she touched a match to the wick and held the candle high in her hand as she ascended. Just as she reached the top of the steps, the light went out.

Nancy's heart began to pound. Was someone up there? She shook off her momentary fear.

"It was only a gust of wind from the open window," she told herself, as she struck an extra match and relighted the wick.

Nancy stepped into the attic. The candle flickered again and nearly went out. Something moved.

"My own shadow, of course," she reasoned. "But how grotesque I look!"

Nancy's eyes focused on a massive wardrobe which stood against the far wall.

"I'll search that first," she decided, crossing the attic.

Setting the candle on the floor, she grasped the knob of the door and pulled.

"Wonder what I'll find?" she asked herself.

The door did not give. At the same moment there was a creaking sound. Nancy could not tell where it had come from. She picked up the candle and looked around.

"It's nothing, I'm sure," the girl assured herself, but she could not shake off the strange feeling that had come over her.

Once more she put down the candle and tugged at the door. It gave suddenly, swinging outward on a squeaking hinge.

From within, a long, bony arm reached out toward Nancy's throat!

CHAPTER VI

A Suspected Thief

NANCY could not stifle a little scream as the long, bony fingers brushed against her throat. She staggered backward. The candlelight flickered wildly.

"We're being attacked by the dead!" shrieked someone behind her.

The voice was Effie's. The maid, worried about Nancy, had followed her to the attic.

"Come away! Come away before that—that thing gets you!" she wailed.

"It's—it's nothing. Nothing but a skeleton," said Nancy, her own voice a trifle unsteady.

"A skeleton!" quavered Effie. "It struck you with its bony hand! Oh, I'm gettin' out o' this house tonight, and I'm never comin' back!" she announced, starting down the steps.

"Please don't go downstairs and frighten Susan," Nancy pleaded, her own momentary nervousness gone. "Surely you see what happened?"

"You were attacked by a skeleton!"

"No, Effie. The thing is hanging inside the wardrobe. One hand seems to be attached to a nail on the door. When I jerked it open, the

50

arm swung out and the fingers touched me.''

To Effie's horror, Nancy reached into the closet and touched the chalk-colored bones. The maid sighed in relief when it did not harm the girl.

"What's a thing like that doing here anyway?" Effie asked in a voice less shaky than before. "I don't like it!"

Before Nancy could reply, they heard slow, measured footsteps ascending the attic stairs. Instantly the maid froze against the wall.

"Someone's coming!" she whispered hoarsely, her feeling of fright returning "We're trapped here!"

"Probably it's Grandfather March," said Nancy, trying to be calm.

Even as she spoke, the old soldier called from halfway up the stairs.

"Anything wrong up there?" he asked. "I heard someone scream."

"We found a skeleton in the wardrobe closet," Nancy explained. "It startled us."

Grandfather March slowly climbed up to the attic and went toward the open wardrobe. In the wavering light of the candle, his shadow moved like that of a misshapen giant.

"Oh, *that* skeleton," he said in relief. "I'd forgotten all about it. Fact is, I didn't know Fipp had put it in the closet."

The elderly man then explained that it originally had been brought there by Dick March, a young medical student and a cousin of Fipp's.

"You know how boys are," he added with a chuckle. "They used this skeleton one Hallowe'en, and Dick never did take it away again."

"You're sure your son put it here?" Nancy asked thoughtfully.

It seemed unusual that anyone would have gone to the trouble of draping the arm on the door, and the Drew girl wondered if there might be any significance attached to the act.

"No, I'm not sure Fipp put it here," Mr. March answered her question. "But who else could have done it?"

Nancy did not reply. Instead she began an investigation of the wardrobe. She figured it was just possible Fipp March had rigged up the strange figure to frighten away all but members of his own family.

Perhaps this was his hiding place for the missing music!

Excited, the girl held up the candle in order to examine every inch of the old piece of furniture. When a hasty glance revealed nothing but dust and cobwebs, she tapped the sides and bottom for sliding panels. None came to light.

Effie, tired of waiting, coaxed Nancy to go downstairs. Grandfather March, concerned about Susan during their long absence, said he thought they all should go below. Nancy did not want to give up the search, but out of deference to the elderly man's wishes, she reluctantly followed the others to the second floor.

"I'm going to look at that old wardrobe again

sometime," she told herself. "I have a hunch it holds a strange secret."

For two hours she and Mr. March talked and listened to the radio. Although Nancy was disappointed that they did not hear the song which he thought was his son's, she did gather a good bit of information about members of the family. The girl concluded that they all had been fine, talented people with a high sense of patriotism. Finally at ten o'clock the elderly gentleman arose and smiled at his guest.

"I believe I shall go to bed now. Thank you very much for everything."

"I wish the mystery were nearer being solved," the girl said, rising also.

Nancy went to the room assigned to her, but she could not sleep. She kept thinking about the skeleton and the man Effie had seen outside the house. Time and again she roused up at unfamiliar sounds on the grounds and in the house. Then all of a sudden she found it was morning and she was waking up.

"Nearly eight o'clock!" she said in astonishment, looking at her watch. "I did get some sleep after all. I believe I'll hurry home and have breakfast with Dad before he goes to his office. And maybe there'll be some mail for me."

Explaining to Grandfather March that she would return later, Nancy drove to the Drew house. There she found her father in his study examining something under a microscope.

"Oh, hello," he greeted her, looking up from

his work and kissing her. "I thought maybe you'd come and eat with your old Dad. Any adventures last night?"

"None, except that a skeleton and I got a little chummy."

"What!"

In the light of day the episode with the medical student's property did not seem so spooky to Nancy. She related the story fully, concluding that she felt sure the wardrobe should be investigated further.

"That attic is a strange place indeed," Mr. Drew commented. Then he turned to a problem of his own. "I'm glad you came back, Nancy, or I believe I would have driven out to get you."

"Anything wrong?"

"Not exactly. But something puzzles me. See these?"

He pointed toward his desk. On it lay two ladies' white silk gloves, which appeared to be identical.

"What in the world are you doing with them?" laughed Nancy.

"Another case," her father smiled. Then he added, "Take a look at these two gloves. Do they appear exactly the same to you?"

Nancy examined them carefully. She replied that she could see no difference between them.

"Nor can I, even under a microscope," declared her father.

"What's the problem?"

"The gloves were manufactured by separate

concerns," Mr. Drew explained. "My client,
Mr. Booker—president of the Booker Manu-
facturing Company—contends that another
company has stolen his secret process for making the special material used in them."

"What's the name of the other company?"

"The Lucius Dight Corporation."

"I know that place!" Nancy exclaimed.
"Mr. Dight's daughter, Diane, was in one of my
classes in school. She's a little older than I am.
You say her father has stolen something?"

Mr. Drew looked concerned. "Is Diane a
friend of yours, Nancy?" he asked.

"No, Dad, I shouldn't call her that. She goes
around with an entirely different crowd.
Diane's an attractive-looking girl but she's
spoiled and willful."

"It's fortunate she's not a particular friend
of yours," Mr. Drew said, much relieved, "because I'd like you to do a little sleuthing for me
on this case."

"I'd love to!"

"I thought so," smiled her father. "I'll tell
you what I heard from Mr. Booker yesterday
afternoon while we eat some of Hannah's good
bacon and eggs."

Father and daughter took their places at the
breakfast table. Then Mr. Drew began his
story.

"My client, Mr. Booker, suspects that a former workman of his, named Bushy Trott, was in
reality a spy from the Dight factory."

"What a curious name—Bushy Trott!"

"His nickname, I assume. I've seen a photograph of the man. A coarse-looking fellow with wild, bushy black hair."

"So Mr. Booker believes that Bushy worked at the plant only to learn the secret process for making the silk material?"

"Yes, his contention is that the man was sent as a spy by Mr. Dight. Before this, the Dight plant manufactured only rayon materials, not silk."

"How can I help on the case?" Nancy inquired eagerly.

"I was wondering that myself, until you mentioned knowing Diane Dight. Do you suppose that through her you might be able to look around her father's plant? As a rule, visitors are barred. If I, a lawyer, should go, the owner might become suspicious of my motives."

"I'll be glad to try!" Nancy offered enthusiastically. "If I get into the factory, what am I supposed to do? Locate Bushy Trott?"

"Mainly that, yes. And if you can observe the process used to make the silk like the material in these gloves, we'll have something to work on," declared Mr. Drew.

"It's a stiff assignment," laughed his daughter. "But no worse than the case of the missing music."

"Have you any clues to that?" asked her father.

Nancy told him what had happened at Pleasant Hedges.

"About all I can say I've done so far is sell a few things for Mr. March," she explained, "and I believe there may be more trinkets up in the old attic. But where the music is hidden, or who the thief may be that stole any of it, is still as big a mystery as ever."

"Perhaps if you work on my case for a while, and then go back to the other one, you'll attack it with a fresh idea," advised Mr. Drew.

After her father had gone to his office, Nancy looked through the mail, but was disappointed to find nothing of special interest. Then she sat down to think about how she might get in touch with Diane Dight without arousing the girl's suspicions as to what could be behind her sudden show of friendship. While she was studying the problem, George Fayne dropped in.

"Why the furrowed brow?" the girl laughed. "Something go wrong? Bet you haven't heard from Ned."

"No, I haven't," Nancy replied, "but what I was thinking about is how I'm going to cultivate Diane Dight."

"Diane Dight! How you can admire that girl is a puzzle to me!" George protested.

"Did I say I admire her?" Nancy countered, her eyes twinkling.

"I might have known," George grinned. "You think she's involved in some mystery. Don't tell me she stole Fipp March's music!"

"No, not that. I'd just like to get her to take me through her father's factory."

"She'd never bother," prophesied George. "Always too busy talking about herself and the latest dress she's having made at Madame Paray's."

"I don't know that dressmaker."

"I do. Mother's having a gown made there to wear to a wedding. It's funny you should mention Diane, because she was there the other day when Mother was, and raised an awful row. Diane wanted Madame Paray to stop all her other work and finish a dress so that she could take it away with her."

"So she isn't in town," said Nancy, disappointed.

"I don't know how long Diane is going to be away. Why don't you phone her house and find out?"

"It would be better if I could get the information some other way."

"How about the dressmaker?" suggested George. "Mother has a fitting there at eleven this morning. Suppose you and I go with her."

"A grand idea."

The two girls hurried off to join Mrs. Fayne. They caught her just leaving the house. A little later Nancy was introduced to Madame Paray. Nancy complimented the dressmaker on Diane Dight's clothes.

"Her figaire ees slim and easy to fit," said the dressmaker modestly. "But I am afraid she diet too much—and ze diet, eet keep you happy or else eet make you cross if you do not eat enough."

"Diane is out of town, isn't she?" Nancy asked.

"She return today on ze two o'clock train. I am afraid zere will be anozzer scene when she come here to get her gown. Eet ees not finish."

Quickly Nancy saw an opportunity to get in touch with Diane. She offered to meet the girl at the station and tell her that the dress was not ready.

"Oh, would you? Zat would be most kind. And please to tell Miss Diane also her papa wishes to hear from her as soon as she arrive."

George grinned broadly. Nancy had made the perfect set-up for herself! After Mrs. Fayne and the two girls left the dressmaker's, George congratulated her friend.

"You're super all right," she remarked. "Worked that just as easy——"

"Worked what?" asked Mrs. Fayne.

"I'm so happy, I'm inviting you both to lunch," grinned Nancy. "Then I'll tell you, Mrs. Fayne, what a schemer I am!"

The meal was a jolly one, and immediately afterward Nancy hastened home to change her clothes. When she came downstairs half an hour later, Hannah Gruen looked at her in amazement.

"Wherever are you going in those party things?" she exclaimed. "And you look years older!"

"I'm going for a drive with the best dressed woman in River Heights—Diane Dight!" Nancy giggled, giving the worthy housekeeper a hug and hurrying away mysteriously. "Please give Dad that message if he should phone," she called from the garage.

She drove immediately to the station. The two o'clock train was just coming in. Quickly Nancy parked the car and dashed across the platform.

The first passenger to step down was Diane Dight. As Nancy went toward the girl, her heart beat faster.

Was her plan going to work?

CHAPTER VII

No Admittance

"Hello, Diane!"

The Dight girl looked up, startled. For a moment she turned pale and barely acknowledged the greeting. As she brushed past, Nancy caught her arm.

"I have a message for you, Diane," she said.

"For me? What is it?" she asked, frightened.

"Madame Paray asked me to tell you that your dress is not ready."

"Oh!" Diane breathed a sigh of relief. Then her eyes snapped. "That woman makes me tired. I wouldn't go to her any more, except—except—that she does make attractive clothes."

"You always look stunning, Diane," said Nancy.

"Thank you," replied the girl.

For the first time she seemed to take note of Nancy's outfit. "I like the dress and hat you have on. Did you have them made?"

"Yes, I did," replied Nancy lightly, stifling a desire to smile. She was thinking how pleased Hannah Gruen would be to hear her handiwork so highly praised. Aloud she said, "I'll drive you home, Diane. Come, let me help you with your suitcase."

Diane protested, but Nancy paid no attention. She took the bag and went to her car. The other girl, instead of thanking her, began complaining about the fact that there were never any porters around and that the family chauffeur was on vacation. When they got into the car, Nancy turned in an opposite direction from the one in which the Dight residence was located.

"Oh, you're going the wrong way!" cried Diane.

"I just recalled that your father wants to see you right away. Madame Paray asked me to give you that message also."

Nancy's plans came near being upset when Diane insisted that she be let out of the car so that she might take a taxi to her father's establishment. Nancy assured her, however, that it would be no trouble at all to drive there, and kept on going until she reached the factory.

There Diane bade her good-by, saying she would go home with her father. But Nancy was not to be put off so easily.

"Oh, I don't mind waiting. There are lots of things I'd like to talk to you about. Suppose I take you home."

The look of dismay which had crossed Diane's face at the railroad station appeared again. Before the girl had a chance to object,

Nancy was out of the car and walking into the building with her. Out of politeness Diane was forced to introduce the Drew girl to Mr. Dight's secretary.

"I don't know how long I shall be with my father," Diane told Nancy, "so don't bother to wait."

After she had disappeared into the inner office, Nancy smiled at Miss Jones, the secretary.

"This must be a fascinating place to work," she said. "Do you know all about the process of making rayon?"

"I know a good deal, but far from everything," the young woman replied pleasantly.

"I should love to go through the plant sometime. Do you suppose Diane would take me?" Nancy inquired.

Miss Jones smiled. "She doesn't seem to be interested in her father's business. If you really would like to take a quick look, I'll show you what I can. Of course, many of the processes used here are kept a secret. Some I do not know myself."

Nancy's pulse leaped. Here was news indeed! She could hardly wait to start her trip through the factory, but she tried to appear calm."

"That's sweet of you, Miss Jones," she said. "If you really can spare the time, I'd love to look around."

"As a rule, visitors are not permitted, but since you are a special friend of Miss Dight's"

—here she appraised Nancy's costume with a complimentary look—"I'll be glad to take you through the plant." As an afterthought she added, "Perhaps we should wait for Miss Dight."

"Oh, let's go now," Nancy urged, fearful that she would lose her opportunity. "There's no telling how long Diane may be with her father."

As she and Miss Jones walked through long halls and up and down flights of stairs, the secretary explained the rudiments of the making of rayon cloth.

"It seems like magic," she said, "to think that giant spruce trees can be turned into lovely soft materials so quickly. First the wood is converted into pulp. Then it is put into those tanks you see over there and churned in a chemical solution for several hours."

"Is the result that orange-colored stuff?" asked Nancy.

"Yes. It's known as cellulose. After that it's dissolved to a form called viscose."

"Nothing very secret about it," thought Nancy.

As Miss Jones led her farther into the plant, the girl kept her eyes open for Bushy Trott. Although there were many workmen busy at their tasks, she saw no one who resembled the suspected thief.

One thing she did take note of was a heavy door on the landing of a stairway at the far end of the building. A metal sign hung on it, saying:

POSITIVELY NO ADMITTANCE.
DANGER. KEEP OUT.

"I wonder if that is one of the secret places Miss Jones spoke about," Nancy speculated to herself. "Maybe Bushy Trott is in there!"

Soon they reached the top of the stairway, and the secretary began her explanation of the next process in rayon making.

"Ahead of you is the machine known as the spinneret," she said. "That is what makes viscose into thread."

"It's remarkable!" Nancy exclaimed, pretending to be watching nothing but this.

At that moment a bell rang several times. The girl wondered what the signal meant.

"That is for me," said Miss Jones. "I guess Mr. Dight wants me. We'll have to go back."

"If you don't mind, I'd like to stay here a little longer," the Drew girl said with a disarming smile. "I'll come down soon."

"Well, I don't know," the woman paused. "You really shouldn't. But stay if you wish. If I see Miss Dight, I'll tell her you're here."

Once the secretary had gone, Nancy did not tarry long in the spinneret room. Instead, she moved quickly down the stairway toward the forbidden room.

"I wish I could look in there," she said to herself.

As Nancy hesitated outside, the door suddenly opened. A workman in soiled dungarees came out, carrying a package which looked as if it might contain a bolt of cloth.

Although the door remained open only an instant, the girl obtained a fleeting glimpse of the interior. She saw several large chemical vats. Beside one of them, his back to her, stood a man with tousled, black hair.

"Bushy Trott!" thought Nancy excitedly. "The spy who worked at the Booker factory!"

The door slammed shut, and she saw no more. Deliberately she loitered until the workman who had come out of the room disappeared down the hall.

"I must get a better look at that fellow with the bushy hair!" she decided. "This is my chance to help Dad solve that mystery!"

Glancing quickly in either direction, Nancy cautiously tried to open the door. To her dismay it had a snap lock and would not budge.

"I must get in there!" In a moment she smiled to herself. "I think I know how to do it!"

CHAPTER VIII

Song of the Wind

PRESSING her lips close to the crack of the door to the secret room, Nancy screamed. The ruse was successful. From within came hurrying footsteps.

The next instant the door swung open. Nancy staggered inside, her hand over her eyes.

"Water," she murmured. "Water."

The big, bushy-haired man who had opened the door stared at her doubtfully. But as the girl repeated her request, he decided something must be wrong.

"Are you sick?" he asked in a coarse, heavy voice.

Nancy did not want to answer questions. To avoid them she pretended to faint. The act was well timed, for the man, frightened, immediately rushed into the hall for help. The young detective smiled.

"I'll bet that's Bushy Trott!" she thought. "When I describe him to Dad, he'll know for sure."

No sooner had the door swung shut behind the fellow than she leaped to her feet. Eagerly she gazed about. The room resembled a laboratory. Near her were several vats of rain-bow-hued solutions.

Nancy had no opportunity to look further. Heavy footsteps warned her that the man was returning. She barely had time to stretch out on the floor before he came into the room.

As the big, burly figure bent over her, the girl pretended to revive. Opening her eyes, she gazed up into his ugly, cruel face. The man's skin was sallow, and his eyes appeared as green as the chemical solution in one of the vats.

"Here, drink this!" he commanded gruffly.

Nancy took a tiny sip of water from the paper cup he offered her.

"I'm feeling better now," she murmured, sitting up.

"How did you get into this part of the factory anyhow? You don't work here. Who are you?" he asked gruffly.

Before the girl could reply, the outside door swung open again. A stout, well-dressed man with piercing brown eyes stepped inside. Seeing Nancy, he paused in surprise.

"Tro——" He stopped, then went on, "What is the meaning of this? Why have you allowed a visitor here?"

"It's none o' my doing, Mr. Dight," his employee muttered. "She came in herself—said she was feelin' sick."

"Then a little fresh air will help you, Miss," said Mr. Dight stiffly.

Taking Nancy firmly by the arm, he assisted

her to her feet, and escorted her down the
stairs into the main section of the factory. He
did not call her by name, and she hoped he had
not been told who she was.

"It is dangerous for you to wander about
this building by yourself. You must never do
it again," he remarked, his tone icy.

Nancy thought Mr. Dight seemed not only
displeased, but also frightened. Had she stumbled upon his secret?

When they came near the main entrance, he
left her. Nancy spoke to Miss Jones and
learned that Diane had left the factory five minutes after reaching it. She had not even both-
ered to wait for Nancy. This surprised the girl,
but she thought little about it at the time. She
said good-by to the secretary, then drove at
once to her own home.

"Dad!" she greeted her father as she ran
into the house. "I had some real luck today!
I think I found Bushy Trott!"

Mr. Drew dropped his newspaper. "Say that
again!" he requested.

Nancy repeated her statement and eagerly
related the entire story of her visit to the Dight
plant. Mr. Drew readily identified the suspect
from Nancy's description of him. He was
deeply impressed with his daughter's work, but
could not hide a smile when he heard of her
ruse.

"Nancy, you're a fast worker and a thorough
one!" he praised her. "If that man actually is

Bushy Trott—and you say Mr. Dight started to speak his name—then the first step in my case appears to have been well taken.''

"What's to be the next move?"

"I'll arrange to have the man watched," Mr. Drew replied. "We'll learn everything we can about him."

"Is there something else I can do?" Nancy asked.

"You've already helped me a lot," her father replied. "If there's anything more, I'll let you know."

Nancy's interest in the case had been aroused, and she wanted to follow it up. But she would be patient. In the meantime, she would devote herself to Grandfather March's problems.

"Watch your step in that old attic," Mr. Drew warned her. "No telling what's up there."

"I promise, Dad," she said, smiling.

The following afternoon found Nancy at the mansion. Susan and her grandfather were listening to the radio in the little girl's bedroom. As Nancy entered, a program of military numbers was on the air.

"Now that's what I call good music!" Mr. March declared, keeping time with his foot. "Puts me in mind of war days."

"Tell Nancy about them, Grandpa!" coaxed Susan.

Grandfather March required no urging. Turning the radio low, he told of some of the stirring experiences he had lived through.

"And show Nancy your medals," Susan demanded proudly.

The elderly man got them from a bureau drawer in his room and explained what they were.

"I'm proudest of this one," he said. "I carried an injured companion across No Man's Land, when shells were popping faster than rain. It saved the fellow's life."

"Where's the soldier's chocolate box?" asked Susan.

"A chocolate box?" inquired Nancy, intrigued.

"One Christmas, Princess Mary sent boxes filled with chocolates and other goodies to many of the English soldiers," Mr. March explained. "A cousin of mine received one, and it came to me when he died. It's one of the things I'll never sell. Just having it keeps me in mind of——"

He broke off suddenly, and with a startled expression moved swiftly to the radio to turn it louder.

"Listen!" he commanded.

The orchestra was playing a gay, new melody now. As the sweet strains continued, Grandfather March cried out:

"That's it! That's one of my son's compositions! I can't remember the name of it."

"It's called *Song of the Wind*," Nancy said, identifying it.

"Who do they say wrote it?" demanded the elderly soldier.

"I can't recall," Nancy confessed. When the composer's name was not announced, she said, "Suppose I run downtown and buy a copy of the song?"

Grandfather March urged her to hurry, and could hardly wait for her return.

"The composer is Ben Banks," she told him as soon as she got back.

"Ben Banks! Ben Banks!" shouted Grandfather March angrily. "Who's he? The man is a thief! That song was Fipp's!"

Thoroughly enraged, the elderly soldier stomped about. Nancy promised to try to locate Ben Banks. She would get in touch with the publisher of *Song of the Wind,* and ask about the identity of the so-called composer.

"I'll never rest until that rascal is found and exposed!" Mr. March stormed. "Why, the upstart! Not only does he rob the dead, but he cheats little Susan out of her rightful inheritance!"

The elderly man's tirade went on and on. To quiet him, Nancy offered to play the selection on the piano, so the two went downstairs to the music room.

As the old piano was badly out of tune, she soon gave this up. She had just begun to sing the lovely song to him, when they were horror-struck to hear a blood-curdling cry for help, followed by a gunshot. Unquestionably the sounds had come from the attic.

Nancy's heart stood still. "Who is up there?" she quavered fearfully, rushing from the room.

"I—I don't know," said Mr. March, his voice shaking with emotion.

He tried to follow, but he was too unnerved. His legs refused to move. He stood as one petrified.

"If Susan—" he whispered.

CHAPTER IX

Black Widow

Nancy raced upstairs. Susan was in her bed, cowering under the covers.

"Thank goodness, she's all right!" thought the Drew girl, speeding on to the attic.

"Who's up there?" she called.

"Me! Effie!"

Nancy doubled her steps. She found the maid alone, jumping about. She was waving her left hand in the air and wailing pitifully.

"I've been bit! I've been bit!" she screamed.

"Bit? Then you weren't shot?"

"I don't know. No, I guess not."

"What bit you?" Nancy demanded.

"The skeleton! Do something, quick!"

"Effie, be sensible. What was it that bit you?"

"It was that skeleton, I tell you!" Dramatically the maid pointed to the bony figure which leaned forward at a rakish angle from the open door of the wardrobe closet. "He just reached out and bit my finger! Oh, the thing is alive!"

Nancy examined the young woman's finger, but in the dim light could see no evidence of a wound. She wondered if the girl's imagination had not got the better of her.

"Who fired the shot?" she asked.

"He did, I guess. That's a live skeleton, I know it!"

Gingerly Nancy looked for a weapon. She found an old rifle lying on the floor beside the wardrobe.

"Is this what went off?" she asked Effie.

"No. Yes. I guess so!" cried the confused girl.

Nancy decided that the rifle must have been propped against the wardrobe and jarred loose by Effie. The question was, who had put it there, and when? She could not recall having seen it before. Had the same person who put the skeleton in place left the death-dealing weapon there too? Nancy was brought out of her reverie by footsteps on the stairway.

"Is that you, Mr. March?" she called. "Don't bother to come up. Everything is all right, I guess."

"Except me," wailed Effie.

"Let's go downstairs," Nancy said to the maid. "I'll examine your finger again. By the way, what were you looking for up here?"

"Some clean linen to change the beds. There's hardly any in the house. Oh, Miss Nancy, my whole arm hurts now."

When they reached the second floor, the Drew girl examined the maid's hand. She received a distinct shock, and Effie herself began to sob.

"Look at it! I'm goin' t' die!" she cried.

This remark brought Susan to the hall. She and her grandfather gazed in awe at Effie's swollen forearm and the tiny puncture in her index finger.

"What is it, Nancy?" the child spoke up in fright.

The girl did not reply. She advised that Susan get back into bed. Quickly she asked Mr. March for a large handkerchief and tied it tightly about Effie's upper arm.

"We'd better run in to a doctor's," she said. "There isn't anything here with which to take care of this wound." To Mr. March she whispered, "I'm afraid a poisonous spider bit Effie."

Nancy drove speedily to the office of Doctor Evans. Fortunately the man was in. He confirmed Nancy's diagnosis, adding that the spider probably was a black widow.

"One rarely finds them in this part of the country," he said, going to a medicine cabinet. By now Effie looked and acted quite ill. "The other spider I don't like is the tarantula, but it isn't native to these parts either," the physician continued.

Effie began to moan, saying she knew her young life was over.

"Nonsense," said Doctor Evans, untying the handkerchief on her upper arm. "Fortunately, Miss Drew put this tourniquet on, and you won't suffer as much as you might have. You'd better keep quiet for a couple of days, though.''

"How am I goin' to do my work?" asked the maid.

"Don't worry about that," spoke up Nancy quickly. "I'll help you."

The doctor gave her some instructions for taking care of Effie, and told the patient not to worry. He also advised that the old house be searched thoroughly for the black widow spider.

"I believe I'll go home and get Mrs. Gruen," Nancy told Effie as they drove off. "She can come out for a few hours to help us."

The Drew housekeeper was glad to be of assistance. As soon as they reached the March homestead, she and Nancy armed themselves with brooms and went immediately to the attic. There they brushed down dozens of webs and caught every spider they could locate.

"We've found none except the common house variety," sighed Nancy at last. "Where *could* the black widow have gone?"

"I'm not going to let you stay here unless we find it," said Hannah Gruen firmly.

Nancy tried to dispel the woman's fears by a light-hearted remark, but actually she was worried. For the second time the thought came to her that someone who had no right to be in the attic had left something there to warn away intruders. First the skeleton, then the gun and the spider.

The most likely person was the one who had stolen Fipp March's original music!

"I must write to the publisher of *Song of the Wind* at once for the address of Ben Banks," Nancy determined. "In all the excitement I completely forgot him."

"Oh!" said Hannah Gruen suddenly.

Crack! Her broom came down with a whack onto a spider which had just crawled from beneath the wardrobe.

"It's the black widow!" cried Nancy jubilantly. "Now you'll have nothing to worry about."

"Unless there are more of these poisonous creatures up here," declared Mrs. Gruen.

She agreed, however, that it probably would be safe for Nancy to stay, but she cautioned the girl to be extra careful.

"I wouldn't want to be accountable to your father if anything should happen to you," she said.

While the housekeeper prepared supper, Nancy hurriedly wrote a note to the publisher of *Song of the Wind,* requesting the address of its composer, Ben Banks. Then she went to make Effie comfortable. The maid was feverish and suffering considerably. When she finally dropped off to sleep, Nancy tiptoed away to see that Susan was all right.

"Nancy, you said spiders were nice, and a bad one bit Effie. She told me."

The Drew girl was provoked to learn the maid had told her, but she merely smiled. "That's right, Susan, but only good spiders live around here. And very few kinds harm people anyway.''

To get the child's mind off the unfortunate subject, she told her about the funny antics of the jumping spiders and the flying variety.

"Some of them are just like trapeze performers in a circus," Nancy explained. "They spin a thread and then let the wind carry them through the air. Sometimes they go all the way from shore to a ship at sea."

"Oh, that kind of a ride would be lots of fun," giggled Susan, her fears gone now.

Hannah Gruen brought up a tray of food for the little girl. Nancy decided that while the child was eating supper, Mr. March might stay with her, and she would drive the housekeeper home. When they reached the Drew residence, Bess and George were just leaving the porch.

"Where in the world have you been, Nancy?" George remonstrated. "We thought something had happened to you. How about having dinner with us at my house and telling us about your new mystery?"

Nancy thanked her friend, but explained why she could not accept the invitation. Bess exclaimed in horror when she heard about the black widow in the attic and the skeleton that seemed to be alive at times.

"You'd better stay out of that place," she advised.

"I'll be careful. Don't worry," Nancy laughed. She told the girls to climb into the car and she would drop them off at the Fayne home.

"If you get bitten like Effie, you won't be able to go to the Emerson dance," said Bess.

"I'm not going anyway," replied Nancy with emphasis. "I've told Horace that."

"And you haven't been invited by Ned Nickerson?"

"No. And please let's forget the whole thing," Nancy pleaded, preferring not to dwell on the subject.

She left the girls at George's house and went on. Although she succeeded in putting the matter of the dance out of her mind by thinking of the two mysteries in which she had become involved, Bess and George continued to discuss the affair for some time.

"I just can't understand Ned," said George angrily. "He must be losing his mind not to have asked the most popular girl who has ever attended an Emerson dance."

She was referring to the time when Nancy had been acclaimed queen for a night at the college.

"Maybe Ned isn't going himself," suggested Bess. "But it's funny Nancy hasn't had a letter or a phone call from him. He used to write rather often."

"There's something strange about the whole thing," declared George. "I feel like calling up Ned and asking him what's the matter."

"Nancy would never forgive you. Maybe

something has happened between them that she doesn't want to tell us about," said Bess wisely.

"If so, it's a shame, because they're both wonderful," her cousin remarked. "I just can't understand it."

Nancy, unaware of her chums' concern, arrived at the March estate in time to tuck Susan into bed. The little girl looked up at her wistfully.

"I wish you'd always stay with me," she confided. "Effie never has time to talk to me and take care of me the way you do."

Nancy leaned down and kissed the child. "I'm going to be here for a while," she promised. "Suppose we pretend each day is a year."

Susan liked this game, and soon she went to sleep happily. Nancy joined Mr. March on the first floor, where he was listening to the radio. As they ate supper together, he told her more about his family.

"I guess my son Fipp came by his musical ability naturally," the elderly man disclosed. "My mother wrote songs for the sheer joy of it. Most of them were composed only for the family and never got beyond manuscript form. My son used parts of the melodies in his work. The piece called *Song of the Wind* was partly based on one that my mother wrote years ago."

Here was a bit of information upon which Nancy pounced eagerly. It might prove to be very good evidence!

"What became of those old songs?" she asked quickly.

"Well, now, I couldn't say. A few of them may have been put away in the attic. I'm sure Fipp didn't have them. The old melodies had been hummed to him so often he knew them by heart."

"If we can find the music, we may have a case against Ben Banks," said Nancy.

The clue was sufficient to start her on another intensive search. As soon as she washed the dishes, she got another flashlight, went to the attic, and began poking around in several as yet unopened boxes. One of these was filled with interesting newspapers, some of which dated back a hundred years.

"I'm reading more than I'm working," the girl chided herself presently with a laugh. "I'd better get on with the hunt."

Going hurriedly through the remaining papers, Nancy came at last to the bottom of the box. Her gaze fastened upon a ribbon-tied roll of parchment.

"This may be the very thing I'm after!" she thought excitedly.

Unwrapping it, she discovered the sheet did contain the music and words of a song. Fipp's grandmother was named as the composer.

"This isn't one of the melodies I've heard," she thought in disappointment, after humming the tune.

She started to investigate another box which

stood near by. As she eagerly plunged her hand down, something sharp buried itself in her finger. With a sinking heart Nancy wondered if she might have been poisoned the way Effie had been!

Gingerly she pushed aside the papers, looking for a black widow. Then she laughed as she saw what had pricked her finger. Shoe buckles!

"What gorgeous ones!" she cried, lifting out several pairs of the old silver ornaments.

They were studded with precious stones, one of which had a sharp prong on it.

"To think men once wore these on their shoes!" Nancy thought in amusement.

She was glad of the find, for she knew the buckles would bring a nice sum for Mr. March. After wrapping them carefully in paper, she put them in her pocket.

At that instant the flashlight which Nancy had laid on the floor went out. As she leaned forward to pick it up, something landed with a soft thud against her hand.

Out of nowhere came floating a few eerie notes of music like the faint strumming of a harp.

CHAPTER X

THE STRANGE SCENT

NANCY, on her knees in the pitch-black attic, kept perfectly still. She hardly breathed. Chills ran up and down her spine.

The music had ceased, but very close to the girl was the faint tiptoeing of stealthy footsteps. These were followed by muffled tapping sounds.

"There isn't a harp or a piano here," Nancy told herself, trying to regain her composure. "Maybe this is another trick, like the skeleton and the gun, to keep people away."

The tapping had stopped now. The girl reached again for the flashlight. This time she found it, but to her dismay it would not go on. She was too far from the stairway to get there safely in the dark among the maze of boxes and trunks.

Suddenly she heard her name murmured. At first the sounds seemed to be right beside her, then faraway and ghostlike.

"Na-a-ancy!"

"It must be coming from downstairs," the girl concluded, as the call became louder. "Thank goodness, now there'll be a light."

She stood up, then froze to the spot as a new thought struck her. If someone really were in the attic, he might harm anyone coming up the steps! Summoning all her courage, Nancy commanded loudly:

"I'm in the attic. Don't come up! Just hold a light for me at the foot of the stairs!"

The girl had half expected a hand to be clapped over her mouth, but nothing happened. In relief she called out again, saying her flashlight was not working.

A few seconds later a light shone up the stairway. Mr. March was speaking to her cheerily. How good his voice sounded!

Nancy gingerly found her way across the attic. Soon she was on the second floor. Grandfather March gave her one look, then took hold of her arm.

"You're white as a ghost," he said. "Something happened. What was it?"

"Did anyone touch the piano downstairs?" she asked him.

"The piano? No. Why?"

"I thought I heard a few notes of music."

"You're not telling me all you know," the elderly man said. "Don't keep anything back."

"I'm afraid somebody or something is in the attic," Nancy admitted. "The place seemed to produce a ghost after my flashlight went out."

Mr. March grunted an "I'll fix him," and started up the stairs. Nancy tried to hold him back.

"I've faced the enemy before," declared the former soldier, holding the candle aloft. "And it's high time I find out about that attic."

Nancy followed him. To her chagrin there was no one above, nor was there any evidence that a person had come into the place by a secret entrance. On the floor near the spot where she had stood lay a large toy bear.

"It must have fallen from the rafters," Nancy decided, telling Mr. March this was one of the strange occurrences during the past fifteen minutes.

"That bear belongs to Susan," explained the elderly man. "I don't know how it got up here."

Nancy was apologetic for having worried him. The girl felt that he thought her fright had come from being alone in the dark.

Nancy said no more about the incident, but she knew that she had not imagined the stealthy footsteps, the tapping sounds, and the musical notes. Who had made them remained a deep mystery.

"Here is a surprise for you," she said, changing the subject. "I located one of the old songs under a pile of newspapers."

Mr. March scanned the parchment eagerly.

"Oh, yes, I remember this," he nodded, humming a few measures of the tune. "My mother composed it. Fipp later added to it and called the composition—let me see—yes, *The Old and the New*. It was one of his finest."

"It's the best find we've made yet," said

Nancy after they had gone downstairs. "If by any chance Ben Banks has published a song with this melody, you'll certainly have a case against him."

"I hope you receive a reply to your letter very soon," sighed Mr. March. "This suspense is rather hard on an old fellow like me."

Nancy spoke a few words of encouragement, showed him the valuable old shoe buckles, then said good night. The next two days kept her busy with the housework, and she had no chance to go to the attic. She spent all her time at Pleasant Hedges, except for a run into the business section of River Heights to see Mr. Faber.

The kindly dealer gave her a good price for the buckles. Mr. March was overjoyed when he learned the amount, but did not forget that the sums of money recently obtained by Nancy could not take care of him and Susan indefinitely.

As soon as Effie felt able to assume the duties of the household once more, the Drew girl returned to her own home. Her father greeted her cheerily.

"Well, I'm glad to see my runaway daughter again," he said affectionately. "I believe I should take the day off and celebrate."

"Let's!" laughed Nancy. Realizing it was mid-morning, she asked, "*Are* you taking a holiday?"

"I'm on my way to see Mr. Booker," the lawyer replied.

Nancy asked her father what progress he had

made in clearing up the mystery of the stolen
formula for creating the lovely silk material.

"Absolutely none," Mr. Drew confessed.
"Men have been shadowing the Dight plant
ever since you were there, but Bushy Trott has
neither gone in nor come out of the building."

"Maybe he sleeps there."

"Or wears a disguise."

"Would you like to have me go back to the
factory and find out?" urged Nancy.

"Not yet, but I may call on you later. Mr.
Booker is so sure his process is being imitated
that whether or not Trott is there, he wants me
to start suit against Mr. Dight."

"Will you do it?"

"Not until I have more evidence," replied
the lawyer. "One has to be mighty careful
when accusing a person of Mr. Dight's standing. Up to now Mr. Booker hasn't explained
much about how he makes the special silk material, so I'm on my way to find out. Want to
go with me?"

"I'll leap at the chance!"

"Then leap right into my car and we'll be on
our way to the Booker factory. Later, if one of
us gets into the Dight plant and sees what's going on in the secret section there, we'll be able
to compare the two methods."

Nancy and her father were welcomed cordially by Mr. Booker, who canceled an important conference to conduct the Drews personally
through his establishment.

"First I'll show you the Gossamer Garment Room," he declared, leading the way.

The name interested Nancy, who wondered what he meant. All she could recall about "gossamer" were bits of poetry about fairies stepping daintily across a carpet of gossamer spider webbing.

"This room contains our finished products," Mr. Booker continued. "Naturally, we guard our secrets well, for if a hint should leak out as to our methods, certain competitors might duplicate our styles and put them on the market ahead of us."

The Gossamer Room contained several bolts of filmy white silk material like that used in the glove Nancy had seen. Others were in various colors, while a few were patterned with artistic and unusual designs.

"They're beautiful!" exclaimed Nancy.

Clever designers had fashioned some of the materials into attractive gowns, which hung row upon row in dustproof glass cases.

"I've never seen anything so lovely!" Nancy said in awe. A pale yellow evening frock caught her eye. "What a stunning dance dress."

In texture it was unlike anything she had ever seen before. "The cloth is strong, yet it looks delicate enough to dissolve at a touch of the hand!" the girl marveled.

"That's why we call it gossamer," said Mr. Booker proudly. "I'll show you how it is made.

You must, of course, agree never to reveal my secrets!''

"You may trust us!" said Mr. Drew.

The factory owner unlocked a heavy metal door and led his callers into a room where two men sat at tables, engaged in a most unusual occupation.

"This is my spidery," explained Mr. Booker. "Here I breed orb weavers under glass. They give me the silk threads I need for my material.''

"You actually use spiders!" gasped Nancy.

"Yes," smiled her guide. "They are very useful to man when one understands how to put them to work.''

Nancy watched curiously. One of the men was holding a spider in a pair of forceps. The little insect was busy exuding a filmy thread from its spinneret. With his other hand the man was winding the silk on a spool.

"The spiders work fast," remarked Mr. Drew.

"One of them can spin a web half a yard across in less than an hour," Mr. Booker revealed. "Now I'll show you how we make the thread strong enough to be woven into cloth.''

Nancy and her father were escorted to the room where the secret chemical formula was mixed. Not only did Nancy look at the solution in the various tubs, but she took particular note of the peculiar scent it produced.

"I'd be more likely to recognize the odor

than anything else. If this chemical is being used at the Dight factory, maybe I can identify it that way," Nancy thought.

Mr. Drew inquired if this was the department where Bushy Trott had worked.

"Yes," Mr. Booker admitted, "he was in this section. He came to me highly recommended as a chemist. Since he left my employ abruptly, I suspect that he was sent here as a spy."

Mr. Drew told the manufacturer he felt better equipped now to carry on his case against the rival concern.

"We're still trying to check on Bushy Trott," he said. "The next step will be to find out how Mr. Dight is making his silk material."

"If only I could get into his factory again!" Nancy remarked to her father as they drove away from the Booker plant.

She felt sure she would recognize the secret process if it were being imitated.

"You couldn't arrange for another trip with your friend Diane?" Mr. Drew smiled.

"She's scarcely a friend, Dad. You recall she walked out on me the other day!"

"Then there must be another way."

"I'll think up something," Nancy promised.

After dropping her father at his office, she had an inspiration. If her scheme should work, she would get into the factory!

Upon impulse she drove directly to the Dight estate to put her plan into action. The grounds were located at the edge of the city and were screened from the road by a high, ivy-covered fence. Nancy turned into the winding driveway and coasted quietly up to the big white house.

Diane, garbed in a long flowered housecoat, was sitting on the steps of the veranda. She was reading a letter. As Nancy stopped the car, the other girl jumped to her feet, startled.

"Hello," Nancy called cheerily. "Did I frighten you?"

"Yes, you did," Diane answered crossly. "Why didn't you let me know you were coming?"

"I didn't know it myself until a few minutes ago."

Nancy leaped from the car. As she came toward Diane, the girl hastily stuffed the letter she had been reading into her pocket. Unnoticed by her an envelope lay on the steps.

Nancy's alert gaze fell upon it, and she gasped in surprise. There was no mistaking either the postmark or the return address in the upper left-hand corner.

"Just a note from a friend," Diane explained quickly, her face turning crimson.

Without allowing her caller a second glance at the envelope, she whisked it away. Nancy's heart began to beat excitedly.

"Diane Dight, of all people to be hearing from that person!" she thought.

CHAPTER XI

A Blue Bottle

"Have you come to see me?" Diane inquired none too cordially.

"I might call it a business trip," replied Nancy. She tried not to show that the letter she had just seen in the other's possession had upset her. "You have a little sister, I believe."

"Jean's ten."

"How tall is she?"

"She comes to my shoulder. Why?"

"She's only a few inches taller than a little girl I know who has very few clothes. I thought your mother might give me a dress or two your sister has outgrown," said Nancy.

"I'll ask her," Diane offered with a shrug. "Come into the house."

This was just what Nancy wanted, since she hoped to see some kind of art object in which the Dights might be particularly interested. If she could obtain something to sell them, she might have a reason for calling on Mr. Dight at his office.

Left alone, Nancy gazed with interest about the luxuriously furnished living room. Against one wall stood a mahogany case with glass

shelves. On them was an array of beautiful old
bottles.

"The very thing!" thought Nancy in delight.

She went over to examine the collection. One
had the face of George Washington etched in it,
another that of Dolly Madison. As the girl
stood gazing at a lovely old blue perfume bottle,
Diane came downstairs.

"There you are," she said, tossing a heap of
garments onto a sofa. "Mother says to take
them all if you like."

Nancy thanked her for the clothing, and then
expressed interest in the bottle collection.

"Oh, that's Mother's hobby," Diane replied
indifferently. "She spends half her time at antique stores trying to pick up bargains. She'd
rather have an old bottle than something new."

"Many old things are far prettier than new
ones," remarked Nancy.

"I don't think so. And especially bottles.
Anyway, one collector in the family is enough."

Nancy was tempted to make a retort, but
wisely kept still. Diane certainly was a disre-
spectful and conceited daughter.

"Thank you for the dresses," she said, gath-
ering them up. "Little Susan will be delighted
to have them."

From the Dight home Nancy drove directly
to Pleasant Hedges. She had seen some old
bottles in the attic there! She found Mr. March
out in the garden, trying without much success
to mow the lawn.

"Isn't that work too hard for you?" Nancy reminded him, pausing.

The elderly man mopped his brow. "I like to keep busy," he said.

"Please let it go and I'll help you later."

Nancy showed Mr. March the dresses she had obtained for Susan. They were very pretty, and gave no evidence of having been worn. The child's grandfather was loath to take them.

"Mrs. Dight was good to send my grand-daughter such fine clothes," he said gratefully, "but I can't accept charity."

"It's not necessary to do that," Nancy returned.

"Then there's some way I can show my appreciation?" he asked.

"Up in your attic are several nice old bottles, way back under the eaves," Nancy told him. "Mrs. Dight collects bottles. I'll see that she gets one, if you like, in return for these dresses."

"Do that. I remember the bottles, now that you speak of them."

"May I sell some of them?" Nancy asked.

"Yes, yes. Every penny helps Susan and me. You might give the blue flowered one to Mrs. Dight."

Excited that her scheme had worked so far, Nancy went at once to the attic. Though the sun was pouring in through the window, she had to turn on her flashlight in order to look in the far corners of the room.

The girl moved cautiously, for she wanted to avoid any further mishaps. Finally, she came to the bottles. There were four large ones and several smaller ones.

As Nancy bent over to pick them up, a board creaked behind her. She straightened up and looked over her shoulder.

"Silly!" she accused herself. "I'm getting jumpy."

The girl lifted up the bottles one by one. The color of the glass told her instantly that they were old and valuable.

"This must be the blue one Mr. March spoke about!" she said, examining it. "It's beautiful. Mrs. Dight is lucky to get this in exchange for a few dresses!"

Placing all the glassware in a box, she started for the stairway.

"Oh, I hope my plan works!" she sighed. "I can accomplish two missions if all goes well! Get some money for Mr. ——"

A sagging board suddenly groaned beneath her. The next instant the piece of old timber gave way. Before Nancy realized what was happening, one foot went through the floor, and she sat down hard.

Twisting as she fell, Nancy tried to hold the precious box so that it would not strike the attic floor. She was not entirely successful, and the next moment she heard the crash of glass.

"Oh, what have I done!" she thought in dismay, entirely forgetting her own discomfort.

Actually she had banged her head on a trunk, skinned an ankle, and bruised an elbow. But her concern was for the bottles. Had she broken them? Had she ruined her chances for putting into effect her plan of getting into the Dight factory?

One by one she lifted out the glass pieces. Two small ones had been smashed, but the others were intact.

"At least I saved the best ones," Nancy told herself. "My, this attic is dangerous as well as spooky."

Stepping carefully to avoid other weakened floor boards, she carried the box downstairs. With Effie's help she washed each bottle until it shone.

"What are you going to do with these?" the maid asked.

"Try to sell them to the husband of a woman who collects old bottles," said Nancy mysteriously.

"You're comin' back tonight?" Effie asked fearfully. "I don't feel well enough to stay here without you, what with ghosts hangin' around the place."

"We haven't seen a real ghost yet," Nancy laughed.

"Call it what you like. You can't fool me," the girl complained. "I see a man prowlin' around, and I'm supposed to believe he was just crossin' the lawn on his way home. Then a skeleton happens to be hangin' in a closet.

How do I know he didn't hang himself there?

"Next a black widow crawls here, all the way from South America maybe, to bite me! And how about that gun? Nobody loaded it, nobody shot it—except a ghost!"

Nancy had to admit there was no sane explanation for what had happened. To allay the girl's fears, she promised to come back and spend the night.

"I'll get here as soon as I can, Effie," she said.

Taking all the bottles with her, she drove to the main highway. There she parked her car and waited for a bus. She had decided that if she should have a chance to investigate the Dight factory secretly, she had better not have her car there as telltale evidence of her presence.

When she reached the plant, it was approaching the closing hour Already workmen were coming through the gates. The Drew girl stopped a minute to look for Bushy Trott, but he did not appear.

"Am I too late to see Mr. Dight?" Nancy inquired anxiously of Miss Jones, the private seccretary.

"He is still in his office," the pleasant young woman replied. "I think he will see you."

She went inside. A moment later she returned to escort Nancy into the private room. Mr. Dight arose as the girl entered, but appeared none too pleased to see her again.

"Mr. Dight, I must apologize for bothering

you," Nancy began, deftly whisking the fine
blue bottle from the box. "I'm afraid I annoyed you the last time I was here."

The factory owner's gaze fastened upon the
beautiful old glass.

"Where did you get that?" he asked in
amazement.

"It's a little gift I brought for your wife, Mr.
Dight. She did a favor for me this afternoon."
Nancy held the bottle so that the sunlight shone
directly through it. "I have several others
here I thought you might like to buy for her collection."

Mr. Dight examined the blue bottle. His cold
manner left him for a moment as he admired it.

"I'll take it to Mrs. Dight. Let me see the
others."

Nancy set them on the factory owner's desk.

"How much do you want for them?" he
asked, the keen, bartering look returning to his
eyes.

"I—I hardly know," Nancy faltered. "They
are rare and valuable."

"Well, state your price," the man said
briskly.

Nancy hardly heard him. She was standing
near an open window. Glancing down into an
alley between the office building and another
brick structure, she noticed a familiar figure.
The man was Bushy Trott!

"I said, name your price," Mr. Dight repeated in an irritated voice.

Nancy did not want to lose her chance of seeing where Bushy Trott was going. Probably he was heading for the secret section where the stolen formula was being used. This was her chance to find out about it!

"Suppose I leave the bottles with you, Mr. Dight," she said hurriedly, moving toward the door. She tried to act as if she were not eager to get away. "No doubt you would like to examine the glassware before deciding what you would want to pay for it."

To the surprise of the factory owner, the girl opened the door and walked out. In a moment she was at the main exit. Hurrying to the alley, she was just in time to see Bushy Trott enter a small brick building.

No one else was in sight. He unlocked the door with a key and passed from view.

"If only I can get in there!" thought Nancy.

Cautiously she tested the door. Although equipped with an automatic lock, it fortunately had not slammed tightly shut. Nancy slipped inside.

The building seemed to be deserted. No voices greeted her ears, nor was there any sound of running machinery.

Moving noiselessly down a narrow hall, Nancy spied Bushy Trott. As the man glanced over his shoulder, she froze against a wall. Apparently he did not see her in the dim light, for he walked on, muttering to himself.

Bushy paused for a moment before another door. Then he quickly let himself inside.

Nancy did not hesitate. As soon as his footsteps died away, she followed him through the doorway. The man was nowhere in sight.

Finding herself in a room filled with vats of liquid, she decided to investigate them. But before she had a chance to do anything, a key grated in a lock.

Ducking behind one of the vats, she again saw Trott, who had let himself in through another door. He did not tarry, and went back into the hall again.

Nancy, relieved, arose and looked into the vats. The color appeared familiar. She sniffed. The odor from the mixture was the same as that which she had smelled at the Booker factory!

"Now I have real evidence," she exulted. "I must get a sample of this!"

Suddenly the girl realized there was another kind of odor in the air. For a moment she thought little of it. Then as it became stronger, her eyes began to water. Her throat had a parched feeling.

"I'd better get out of here!" she decided, holding her breath. "Some kind of gas is escaping!"

Quickly she went to the hall door. It was locked and would not open from the inside. Nancy raced across the room. The second door would not yield.

Her lungs bursting, the trapped girl tried the third and last door. She had no success.

"That high window—" she thought in desperation, trying to reach it.

Nancy could hold her breath no longer. With a gasp she filled her bursting lungs with the poisonous air.

Objects danced crazily before her eyes, then slowly faded away. Tiny bells tingled in her ears. She groped again for the window. Missing it, she slumped to the floor where she lay unconscious.

CHAPTER XII

A Night Prowler

AFTER Nancy's sudden departure from the office, Mr. Dight spent twenty minutes examining the interesting collection of antique bottles. At the end of that period he rang impatiently for his secretary.

"What became of that girl who was here?" he demanded.

"I really can't say, Mr. Dight," replied Miss Jones. "She left the building without any explanation."

"Left the building, eh?" speculated the factory owner. "Who is she?"

"A friend of your daughter's. Her name is Nancy Drew."

"Don't know her."

When Mr. Dight reached home, he handed his wife the lovely old blue bottle which Nancy had sent to her. She exclaimed over its beauty and at once gave it a conspicuous place in her collection.

"Who is this Nancy Drew?" Mr. Dight asked his daughter.

"Oh, don't you know?" said Diane. "Her father is a lawyer."

"Carson Drew?"

"Yes."

Mr. Dight gave a start.

"Nancy thinks she's a detective," said Diane disparagingly.

"A detective!"

The factory owner looked worried. He recalled how he had found Nancy in the "No Admittance" room of his plant a few days before. And she had disappeared rather abruptly this very afternoon. Mr. Dight went to the telephone and called a number not listed in the directory. It rang in the small red brick building. There was no answer.

"Where is Trott?" he wondered.

Mr. Dight next got in touch with the night watchman through the regular office telephone. O'Dooley answered promptly.

"What's that you say? Look around for a girl in the factory? I'll be afther doin' that, boss."

"Call me back as soon as you find out anything."

In a little while O'Dooley reported no girl had been seen anywhere. Mr. Dight sighed in relief.

"Probably she went home," he thought, but later telephoned the Drew residence to be sure.

Hannah Gruen, deeply worried because of Nancy's long absence, answered the summons. "No, Miss Drew hasn't come in yet this evening," she revealed.

The call from Mr. Dight added to the house-

keeper's uneasiness. As the night wore on, she
tried several times to contact Carson Drew.
The lawyer was out of town on a business trip,
and did not expect to return until nearly midnight. He could not be reached by long distance.

"Nancy must be at the Marches," Hannah
reasoned. "But it's not like her to stay there
without telling me."

The telephone rang. The woman leaped to
her feet and took down the receiver hopefully.
To her bitter disappointment the call was not
from the girl. Instead, it came from Horace
Lally.

"I want to talk to Nancy," he said in an important way. "She wrote me a letter saying
she was too busy to come to the Emerson dance
with me. What's she doing that takes up so
much of her valuable time?"

"You'll have to discuss your problem with
her," Mrs. Gruen cut him short. "I'm busy
and worried. I haven't a minute."

Horace, always curious, tried to learn why
the housekeeper was so upset. Mrs. Gruen
wisely did not reveal that Nancy was missing.

At the March homestead, Effie too was grow-
ing alarmed because the Drew girl had failed
to come there to spend the night. Every time
she heard a car on the road, she would listen
and wait for it to appear, pressing her face
against the windowpane and peering out
through the dark pines.

"Nancy never **broke** a promise to me before," she wailed. "She knows I'm scared to stay here at night without her."

At nine o'clock Effie decided that it would be futile to wait longer for the girl. Reluctantly she went to the room she was sharing with Susan and prepared for bed. As she did not want to awaken the little girl by putting on a light, she undressed in the darkness, glancing around nervously as she did so. Each shadow in the room took on the appearance of something alive.

"What a dark, ugly night," the maid observed, looking out of a window. "Not even a moon——"

Her thoughts on the weather ended abruptly. Beneath the window there moved a stealthy, indistinct figure. Someone was creeping along the high, untrimmed hedge which ran beside the wing of the rambling house!

Effie tried to scream, but no sound came from her throat. She recoiled a step from the window. When she regained her courage sufficiently to look out again, the man was gone.

Terrified, the maid leaped into bed. For a long while she lay absolutely still, the covers pulled up to her ears.

"I locked all the doors and windows before I went to bed," she encouraged herself. "A body couldn't get into this place—or could he?"

A sudden sharp breeze rattled the windows. Overhead timbers groaned.

"Now was that the wind, or was it someone

walkin' over a loose board?" Effie speculated. "Oh, me! Why did I ever come to this place?"

The maid could not sleep. She was convinced that the man she had seen outside had slipped into the house.

"Maybe he knows a secret way to get in," Effie tormented herself. "Maybe he's in the house right now! Oh, gracious, what was that?"

Distinctly she heard a door down the hall open with a squeak. Then footsteps with measured tread came along the hall.

Effie could bear the suspense no longer. Though frightened half out of her wits, she tiptoed to her bedroom door and opened it a crack. A man in a long dark robe, candle in hand, walked toward her.

"Oh, it's you, Mr. March!" exclaimed Effie in relief, recognizing him in a moment. "I thought it was someone else sneakin' along the hall!"

The elderly man held his candle high.

"There's no one here now," he said. "You'd better go back to bed, Effie."

"I can't sleep for thinkin' of Miss Nancy," the maid wailed. "She promised to come back tonight. Oh, I hope nothing has happened to her!"

"Probably something came up, and she couldn't get here," Mr. March tried to reassure Effie. "And of course she couldn't telephone to us."

Relieved, the maid returned to her bed and immediately dropped into slumber. She would not have slept so well had she known that Mr. March was not the mysterious prowler she had heard; in fact, he himself had awakened to hear footsteps somewhere above. Not wishing to alarm the nervous maid further, he wisely had kept the knowledge to himself.

"I wish Nancy Drew had stayed here to-night," he muttered as he went toward the attic. "That girl is so level-headed——"

Grandfather March warily climbed the stairs and looked around. There did not appear to be anyone on the third floor. He poked among the various boxes and trunks, but found nothing suspicious.

"Nevertheless, both Effie and I heard sounds," he kept telling himself.

He finally went downstairs and got back into bed, but he could not sleep.

Meanwhile, at the Dight factory, the search for Nancy had been abandoned after the watchman had reported he could not find her.

"She may have gone to that child Susan's house," Diane suggested to her father.

Mr. Dight hoped his daughter was right and that the girl detective was not in the factory. Actually, at that very moment, Nancy was lying unconscious in his laboratory, her eyes closed and her face pale as death.

For a while she did not stir. Then, as the

suffocating fumes in the room gradually cleared away, she slowly opened her eyes and looked around.

Though Nancy did not know it, she owed her very life to the man she had pursued—Bushy Trott. In passing through the hall shortly after Nancy had been overcome, he had detected the odor of escaping chemical fumes. Alert to danger, he had entered the room, turned off a cock, quickly raised a window, and departed without noticing the girl lying inert on the floor.

The sudden rush of fresh air helped to revive Nancy. She stirred and groaned as her senses began to return.

Trott, far down the hall, heard the sound. He paused alertly.

"What was that?" he asked himself.

The groan was repeated.

"Why, that sounded as if it came from the chemical-mixing room!" thought Trott. "But no one could be in there! Or has someone sneaked in to spy on me?"

Mystified and decidedly worried, he went back to investigate.

CHAPTER XIII

LOCKED IN THE FACTORY

BUSHY TROTT walked swiftly to the chemical-mixing room of the factory. Unlocking one of the doors, he peered inside. He could see no one; nor did he hear any sound save the steady drip, drip of a water faucet. Convinced that he had imagined hearing the groans, he locked the door once more and left the building.

Somewhat later, Nancy fully regained consciousness. It was dark in the laboratory now. Sitting up, she tried to figure out where she might be.

The girl could feel a cool breeze blowing across her face. Her head ached, and she barely kept her balance as she rose slowly to her feet.

"Oh, now I remember!" Nancy thought. "I'm locked inside the Dight factory! Yes, I inhaled poisonous fumes. I'm lucky to be alive!"

Nancy stumbled about the dark room in search of an exit. For a time she forgot that all the doors were locked. At last her hand came in contact with an electric switch which she flicked. But no light came on.

"There must be another switch somewhere," she reasoned.

Still unsteady on her feet, Nancy groped her way along the rough plaster wall. Her fingers approached an open ventilator shaft. Through it was crawling a large, deadly spider —a black widow!

Nancy stumbled on, feeling her way. Closer and closer she came to the spider. In another moment her hand would touch it!

Just then she bumped her head against a swinging light. Reaching up, she turned it on.

Over her shoulder Nancy saw the black widow. In horror she backed away. The sight of the spider brought back her dulled faculties completely. In a moment she had killed it with her shoe.

"How did that deadly thing get in here?" she gasped.

As she glanced toward the ventilator, her question was answered.

"It probably crawled through there!" she thought with a shudder. "What's in there?" Then an idea came to her. "Maybe Bushy Trott uses spiders to make silk thread like Mr. Booker does."

Excited, she looked through the ventilator. It was dark beyond, but Nancy found a switch which lighted the inner room. It was filled with glass cases, but she could not see what was in them.

"I must find out if they house spiders," she decided. "If so, that will be another bit of evidence against Mr. Dight."

Near the ventilator was a door which apparently led to the room. To Nancy's annoyance it had no knob or visible lock, nor could it be pushed or pulled.

"It must open by means of a secret spring," she reasoned.

With infinite patience the girl moved her hand over every inch of the panel. Suddenly, for no apparent reason, the door swung inward.

"I must have touched the spring!" she thought gleefully. "Anyway, I'm inside!"

Scarcely had the door closed behind her than the night watchman, attracted by the light she had turned on, came to investigate. Although he had no keys to the laboratory, he stood for a long while in the yard, gazing up at the window.

"Someone is in there!" he muttered. "I'm going to telephone Mr. Dight!"

Nancy, meanwhile, was cautiously exploring the inner room of the laboratory. A quick glance at the cases told her that they contained spiders. But they were not the harmless orb weavers like those at the Booker factory. They were black widows!

"They're just as useful for thread, and I suppose that's why they're here!" thought Nancy. "Bushy Trott has nerve to work with the poisonous things. I wonder what Effie would say to that."

Effie! Nancy suddenly recalled her promise to go back to Pleasant Hedges. She glanced at her watch and was startled to see how long she had been in the laboratory.

"I must get a sample of the chemical solution in the other room, and then find my way out of here," the girl decided.

Unknown to her, the night watchman was at that moment telephoning to Mr. Dight.

"A light is burning in the secret laboratory, boss," he reported excitedly. "Someone must be up there prowlin' around."

"Keep watch of the exits," Mr. Dight ordered. "I'll be right over."

Diane had overheard the telephone conversation.

"Is Nancy Drew at the factory?" she asked, concerned. "Oh, Father, whatever you do, don't let reporters hear about it!"

"Reporters!" snapped Mr. Dight, reaching for his hat. "I've more serious concerns than newspaper stories!"

"It's important," wailed his daughter. "Oh, please promise me there will be no publicity."

"Why should you care?" demanded her father.

Diane was without an answer, but only for a second.

"Nancy is a good friend of mine," she answered glibly. "I don't want to embarrass her."

"We'll spare her feelings," Mr. Dight replied, as he hurried to his waiting car. "The important thing, if she is at the factory, is to get her out of the place before she learns **too many** secrets!''

Never suspecting that the factory owner was en route to the plant, Nancy sought a sample of the chemical mixture. She was in the outer section of the laboratory now, hunting in vain for a container. The shelves were lined with bottles, but all were filled with fluids.

''I know!'' Nancy chuckled. ''Why didn't I think of it before?''

In her pocket were two miniature bottles, part of the March collection. She had intended to offer them to Mr. Dight, but in her haste to leave his office she had forgotten to do so.

Though small, each tiny receptacle was provided with a stopper. Taking care not to dampen her fingers, Nancy filled the containers from two different tanks.

Suddenly she heard whistling outside the building. Was someone watching her? What should she do? Turn off the light or leave it on?

Nancy decided to leave it on, but escape as quickly as possible. Then she remembered that the doors would not open without a key. Recalling there was an exit inside the spidery, she decided to take a chance on that one.

Again she worked on the secret spring, and somehow managed to open the door. As she slid through, Nancy heard the squeal of car brakes outside. Then came the sound of running footsteps.

In panic the girl sped to the door at the far end of the spidery. She felt a momentary sense of helplessness when it would not yield; but with an extra tug it opened.

A steep flight of steps led downward. A rush of damp air from below encouraged her to hope that it might have come from out-of-doors.

Nancy was so desperate that she felt willing to accept almost any risk. Groping her way along, she crept down the steps. Below was a dark, musty cellar.

"Trapped again!" she thought in despair.

She took a few steps, only to bump her knee against a glass-covered case. There seemed to be hundreds of them all about her. She wondered if they contained black widows.

"I'll go back where I was," she thought, retreating. "I'd rather be caught than bitten!"

Nancy could not find the stairway leading upward. As she groped for it, she became aware of a cool breeze blowing across her face.

"That's fresh clean air!" she told herself, trying to be calm. "This cellar must have an outside exit!"

Inching her way along, Nancy followed the stream of air. Not far ahead she saw a dim patch of light. Stumbling toward it, she came to the entrance of a low tunnel with a tiny electric bulb above it.

"This must be the way out!" she decided.

Bending over, Nancy crept along the tunnel. Several times she heard creepy noises, and once her hand encountered something cold and slimy. Without pausing to find out what it was, she hurried on.

The tunnel was not long. Soon the floor began to slope at a steep angle. Another dozen yards, and Nancy came to a heavy door with a small barred opening in it. The door was bolted but she unlocked it without difficulty. Swinging it inward, she climbed a flight of stone steps to an alley.

"Free!" she congratulated herself. "But what an awful adventure I've had!"

Nancy stood for a moment by the factory wall. Breathing deeply of the night air, she sought to get her bearings. Some distance away the girl saw a street lamp and a main thoroughfare. She reasoned that it must be at the south boundary of the plant.

Nancy started forward, but immediately paused. A man had just entered the alley. His head was held low, and she could not see his face. His walk, however, was decidedly familiar.

"That looks like Bushy Trott!" she thought in panic. "If he catches me here, all of my night's work may be a total loss!"

CHAPTER XIV

An Underground Escape

FEARING she might be seen by the man she thought was Bushy Trott, Nancy looked about frantically for a hiding place. There was none in the alley. She did not want to go back to the cellar.

"Perhaps he won't notice me behind this gasoline drum!" she thought hopefully. It was the only place she could find to hide.

The alleyway was dark, lighted only by the far-off street lamp at the entrance. Crouching behind the drum, Nancy waited.

The man came nearer. He passed within a foot of the worried girl but did not see her. Suddenly he pulled off a mustache and a wig. He was Bushy Trott!

The burly fellow descended into the cellar passageway. A moment later Nancy heard the dull click of a latch as the heavy door swung shut.

"Lucky I didn't hide down there!" she thought. "Now to get home!"

Once out in the street, Nancy looked for a cab, but it was ten minutes before she found one. In a short time she was at her own residence. Through an unshaded window in the living room, she could see Hannah Gruen talking excitedly to her father. He was pacing the floor nervously.

"Dad is home from his trip," Nancy reflected, hurrying up the steps. "Wonder if he's worried about me?"

She pushed open the front door and hurried inside. Her unexpected appearance caused Mr. Drew and the housekeeper to gasp with astonishment. The lawyer threw his arms about his daughter.

"Nancy! Nancy! You're safe!" he cried.

Mrs. Gruen was equally effusive. "I've been so terribly worried about you," she said, wiping away her tears. "Where *have* you been?"

With a great sigh, Nancy dropped to the sofa. Now that the strain was over, she realized how utterly exhausted she was.

"I've had a perfectly awful experience," she confessed. "I was locked up in the Dight factory."

"The Dight factory!" exclaimed Mr. Drew. "I had no idea you had gone there."

"Mr. Dight has a room where he keeps black widow spiders. One of the horrible things almost bit my hand. But it was good that I went there, just the same."

"I shudder to think of your taking such risks to help me in my work, my dear," her father said, sitting down beside her. "Tell me everything."

His daughter removed the tiny bottles of

fluid from her pocket and carefully placed them on a table. "Here are samples of the solution in Mr. Dight's private laboratory. It certainly looks as if he had copied Mr. Booker's method of making the beautiful silk thread."

"I'll take this sample to Mr. Booker tomorrow!" exclaimed the lawyer. "If it proves to be the same formula as his, then I can start my case against Mr. Dight."

Kindly Hannah Gruen, concerned over Nancy's paleness, asked Mr. Drew if he would mind hearing the rest of his daughter's story in the morning.

"Oh, I'm thoughtless," the man said instantly. "Of course, Nancy, you must get right to bed. Perhaps I should call Doctor Evans. Those poisonous fumes——"

"Sleep will fix me up," the young detective smiled wanly. "And a glass of hot milk."

As Nancy climbed the stairs to her room, Hannah hurried off to get the milk. In a few minutes the housekeeper was tucking her in, just as she had done when Nancy was a little girl.

"You haven't told me whether there were any letters for me, or any phone calls——"

"Nothing of importance. Horace Lally phoned," Hannah replied.

"What—did he—want?" Nancy's eyes were closed.

"He still wants you to go to the dance with him."

The girl drifted off into slumber. It seemed

as if Ned Nickerson were sailing into the clouds with her. A wicked bird was pursuing them. Its face was Horace Lally's!

Nancy's dream changed suddenly. She was swimming about in a vat of chemical fluid and could not get out. Bushy Trott was leaning over the edge of it, gloating. Suddenly an aviator parachuted right through a window and rescued her. He was Ned Nickerson!

At last Nancy fell into a peaceful sleep from which she did not awaken until eleven o'clock. As the girl opened her eyes, she noticed that someone was peeking at her from the doorway.

"I'm awake, Bess," Nancy called cheerily. "Come in."

Bess Marvin walked in, smiling, and plunked herself down on the bed. "How do you feel?"

"All right, I guess. I'm glad to see you. What's going on? I feel as if I'd been out of circulation for a month!"

At this moment George Fayne came galloping into the room.

"Hi, Nance!" she said, grinning. "Gee, I'm relieved to see you're okay. Mrs. Gruen had me scared last night."

"How?"

"She called up our house to see if you were there and hinted you were missing."

" 'Chickens always come home to roost,' " quoted Nancy with a laugh.

"Unless they get their heads chopped off in the meantime," said George. "And say, maybe you'll want to chop my head off when you hear what I did for you."

"Now, George——"

"Anyway, I think I knocked the conceit out of Horace Lally."

"What are you talking about?" Nancy demanded.

George looked at Bess. "Shall I tell her?"

Bess shrugged. "I've said all along she ought to go."

"Please," Nancy begged.

"Well, while we were waiting for you to wake up—to see if you were all right," George began, "the telephone rang, and I answered it. Horace was on the wire. I said he couldn't speak to you. Then he asked me if I would try to persuade you to go to the dance with him."

"You didn't agree?"

George hedged about replying. "Nancy, he's really crazy about you. When I asked him what gave him the idea you might go with him, he lost all his conceit. In fact, he seemed pretty humble."

"I can't imagine Horace being humble," smiled Nancy. "But, George, you shouldn't have said that."

"Nevertheless, when Horace began to say such wonderful things about you, I—" George paused. "I told him I'd try to get you to go to the dance with him."

Nancy's feelings were mixed. She appreciated her friend's desire to help her have a good time. She even decided that perhaps Horace was not as bad as she had pictured him. Still, she did not want to go with him.

"Isn't Horace Lally a cousin of Diane Dight's?" Bess asked abruptly.

"I believe he is."

"By the way, how are you making out with Diane?" George inquired.

"She gave me several pretty dresses for Susan." Out of deference to her father, Nancy thought it best not to reveal what she had learned at the Dight factory. She added lightly, "I'm sure Diane and I never will be close friends, though."

Hannah Gruen appeared in the doorway at that moment with a tray of food. "Good morning, Nancy," she said. "It's high time you had a square meal."

The girl hopped out of bed. "Let me wash first and brush my teeth. Um, that bacon——"

On the tray lay a letter from the Jenner Music Publishing Company of Oxford. Nancy explained to the girls that she had written to the firm several days before to ask for information regarding the composer Ben Banks. Eagerly she tore open the envelope and read aloud:

Dear Miss Drew,

Your letter interested us very much. We regret that we are unable to provide any of the information you request concerning Ben Banks, whose songs we publish.

> Very sincerely yours,
> Milton Jenner
> Jenner Music Publishing Company.

"What an unsatisfactory answer!" Nancy cried impatiently. "I'm going to write at once and ask for a personal interview."

As soon as she had finished her breakfast-lunch and had dressed, she sat down to write another letter to Mr. Jenner. In it she hinted that there was a matter of vital importance she would like to discuss with him.

"Come with me while I mail this," she said to Bess and George. "And how about going out to Pleasant Hedges with me for the night? Effie ought to have some time off."

"That place is anything but pleasant," remarked Bess. "It gives me the creeps."

"Oh, a ghost or two won't hurt you," laughed George. "Let's go."

"I'll meet you girls at the bus terminal at four o'clock," said Nancy. "My car is parked out in the country."

During the afternoon the Drew girl did several errands, including buying supplies for the March household. On an impulse she stopped in the leading music store and asked for copies of all the songs composed by Ben Banks.

"There are only three," the clerk told her.

"*Song of the Wind* and these other two. They're newer.''

''When were they published?''

''Very recently. They came out one right after the other. Ben Banks must be a clever person to compose so many grand songs in such a short time.''

Nancy thought this sounded very suspicious. She sat down at the piano in the store and played the two selections she had not heard before.

''You do all right, Miss,'' the clerk complimented her.

Nancy smiled, paid for the music, and left the shop. Her mind was working fast. She was sure Grandfather March had whistled parts of the melodies she had just played. Then a sudden thought struck her.

''If Ben Banks stole them from Fipp March, I wonder if his publisher knows it,'' she mused.

At four o'clock Nancy met Bess and George. After a bus ride of several minutes, they picked up the Drew girl's car where she had left it on the road the day before and drove to the March mansion. Effie greeted them at the door.

''Oh, Miss Nancy, you're all right!'' she cried out. ''I was scared somethin' had happened to you when you didn't come last night. You never broke a promise before. And dreadful things were goin' on here.''

Nancy's heart sank until she learned that the ''dreadful things'' were merely the prowling figure outside and the creaking boards overhead.

"Ain't that enough?" asked Effie, when Nancy did not become excited.

"I'm sorry you didn't sleep well," said Nancy. "Tonight you go to the movies and then home to your own bed. We'll stay here."

"Glory be," said Effie in delight, hurrying off to change her clothes.

While Bess and George started preparations for supper, Nancy sought out Mr. March, who was trying to seal up a crack in the second floor hall.

"I have something to show you," she said, spreading out the music on a deep window sill for him to see. "Does this look like your son's work?"

"Now bless you, I wouldn't know!" exclaimed Mr. March, peering at the sheets. "All that looks like Greek to me! I can't sing a measure of music without a piano to help me out."

"I'll sing the melodies to you," Nancy offered.

After hearing them, the elderly man cried out, "Yes, those are Fipp's songs! I'd like to go into court and face that rascal Ben Banks!"

Nancy told him about the letter she had received and of the reply she had sent.

"Good," he said. "Those songs belong to the Marches, and I want the world to know it!"

"I wish I could find some definite proof before I meet Mr. Jenner," said Nancy. "To-morrow the girls and I will hunt some more."

Supper was a delicious meal, with several tasty surprises. Grandfather March was delighted.

"This seems like old times," he chuckled. "It's like one of the old family dinner parties we used to have."

Immediately after supper, Nancy put Susan to bed. But the child was not sleepy. She begged for one story after another.

"Tell me about a king," she said.

"Well, once upon a time——"

"Yes," Susan prompted.

"King Bruce of Scotland——"

Her voice trailed off. Susan noticed that Nancy's attention was focused on the garden.

"Why don't you go on?" the little girl asked impatiently. "Do you see something?"

Nancy did not reply. Jumping quickly to her feet, she moved closer to the window. The hour was well past eight o'clock and dusk had settled over the garden.

In the gleam of light from the kitchen windows she saw the bushes move. As they were parted, the dark, shadowy figure of a man glided forward.

"I'll be back in a minute," Nancy said to Susan.

Telling no one what she intended to do, she hastened outdoors in pursuit of the prowler.

CHAPTER XV

SMOKE!

NANCY went quickly out of the front door. In the dusk it was not easy to distinguish objects, but she dimly saw a man in a felt hat, pulled low, disappearing around a corner of the house. By the time she reached the spot, he had vanished.

"Now where did he go so quickly?" she asked herself, perplexed.

Putting her ear to the ground, she listened attentively for footsteps. She could hear none.

"He must have gone into the house," she speculated excitedly. "But where?"

Cautiously she circled the old mansion, looking at each darkened window for a telltale light. None appeared.

"If that man is in the house, he must know his way around in the dark!" the girl thought. "I must warn the others."

In haste Nancy went inside. She spoke first to Bess and George, who were still in the kitchen.

"I—there is a prowler around," she said breathlessly. "Will you please post yourselves outdoors and yell if you see him leave the house?"

"Where are *you* going?" demanded George.

"To the attic."

"Not alone?" quavered Bess.

"I'll get Mr. March."

The elderly soldier was considerably upset by Nancy's announcement. After making sure that Susan was all right, they tiptoed to the door which opened onto the attic stairway. Very gently Grandfather March turned the key.

As he did so, there came distinct creaking sounds from somewhere overhead. This was followed by the same harplike notes Nancy had heard once before.

The door was open now. There was no sign of a light above. Nancy and Grandfather March waited. Complete silence.

The stillness was broken by Susan. Afraid, the child had come into the hall. Seeing the listening figures, she sped toward them, crying:

"What's the matter? Are you going up to the attic?"

For a second Nancy was provoked that the child had spoiled her plans. Then the girl had an idea of how she might put Susan's words to good use. She said in a loud voice:

"Get into bed, dear, and we'll tell you a story."

She motioned to Grandfather March to take the little girl away. Nancy herself took his flashlight, and noiselessly stepped to the stairway. She closed the door behind her with a bang.

"If that man is in the attic, I hope he thinks I went the other way," she reflected.

For several minutes she waited. No light appeared above her. There were no sounds except the rumble of Mr. March's voice, as he sought to calm Susan with a story.

Finally Nancy inched her way upward, testing each step for creaky spots before putting her weight on it. Reaching the top stair, she held her flashlight at arm's length, then clicked it on. Quickly she played it over the entire attic.

"No one here now," she decided. She sniffed suddenly. "Smoke!" she murmured.

Nancy's heart leaped wildly. Was the place on fire?

She sniffed again. No, not a fire, but someone had been smoking recently in the attic!

At that instant Grandfather March called sharply:

"Nancy!"

"Yes?"

"You're all right?"

"Yes. I didn't find anyone here."

The elderly man started up the steps. "I had no idea you were going to the attic alone," he scolded. "I thought you just meant to hide until I could get back."

Before Nancy had a chance to reply, there came a shout from the garden.

"Bess and George must have seen the man," the girl cried, hurrying down the steps.

She raced every foot of the way to the front door. Her friends were speeding through the pine grove toward the main road. Nancy took after them as fast as she could.

Suddenly she became aware that a figure was running directly toward her. A man! Here was her chance to nab the intruder! Nancy hid behind a tree.

"As soon as he reaches here, I'll——"

Her plan of capture failed, for Bess and George, having discovered him doubling back, had changed their own course. The suspect, who carried a rolled paper in his hand, veered to the right. Nancy started after him.

The man must have heard her, because he looked back for a second. Then he shot ahead and out of sight. As Nancy sped forward, she met her chums.

"Where'd he go?" cried George.

"This way."

Nancy led the chase which ended abruptly a short distance from the main road. Their quarry apparently had jumped into a car and gone off, for the girls heard a motor start and in a moment saw a red tail light disappearing around a bend.

"If that isn't the worst luck!" cried George. "We almost had him."

"It's a shame," said Nancy. "Did you get a good look at him?"

"No, it was too dark," Bess replied. "He seemed to sneak out of nowhere so unexpectedly."

"Did he come from the house?" Nancy asked.

"We don't know. All of a sudden there he was, just ahead of us. When George yelled, he started to run."

Grandfather March met the girls at the front door. He had been torn between two desires: he had wanted to help in the chase, but the fresh excitement had frightened Susan anew, and it seemed better that he stay with her.

It took Nancy half an hour to quiet the little girl. When she finally became calm, the child reminded the Drew girl that she had not finished her story.

"Tell me about King Bruce of Scotland," Susan begged, but followed her request with a yawn.

"Tomorrow, dear."

"Please," she asked. Her eyes were closing.

"Well, King Bruce was a very nice man and all the people loved him——"

Nancy stopped. Susan was asleep. The storyteller tiptoed away and closed the door. As she went downstairs, the girl recalled the rest of the story of how indirectly a spider, through the lesson it taught in perseverance, had saved Scotland. She smiled determinedly.

"If Bruce could lose his kingdom, be imprisoned by enemies, and then find a way to escape and restore his people to power, all because he watched a hard-working spider," thought Nancy, "I guess I shouldn't be discouraged about this mystery!"

So far she had met nothing but failure. But

on the next attempt maybe success would come to her. She would try harder than ever!

In the dining room Bess had turned on the radio, "to restore her courage so she would dare to stay in the spooky old house," as she put it. Mr. March suddenly jumped up from his chair.

"They've done it again!" he cried.

"Done what?" exclaimed Bess.

Before he could reply, the music died away. From the loudspeaker came the announcer's clear, crisp voice. Nancy fully expected to hear the name Ben Banks. Therefore, she was startled at what she did hear.

"You have just listened to a new composition by Harry Hall. This completes the program of the Magic Hour. Listen in again tomorrow at this same time——"

Grandfather March angrily snapped off the switch.

"I'll do more than listen!" he fumed. "Harry Hall indeed! My son wrote that, every note of it. If I can only scrape together a few dollars, I'll take the case to court. I'll show those thieves a thing or two!"

Then, remembering that he had no evidence in support of his case, he sat down utterly dejected. Nancy tried to encourage him.

"Is there anyone besides your family who has heard Fipp play the songs? Anyone who might positively identify him as the composer?"

Mr. March shook his head. "There's no one I know of," he admitted. "Mrs. Peabody used to come to the house to hear Fipp play the piano, but she died last year.''

"Didn't Fipp have any younger friends?"

"Plenty of them, but they've scattered to the far corners of the earth. I wouldn't know where to find them.''

Nancy tried a different approach. ''Are you certain that your son never sold any of his songs?''

"Fipp wouldn't sell his music. He composed it because he loved to. I'm sure he would have told his wife Connie if he had sold any of his songs.''

Although she did not tell Mr. March, Nancy was afraid another piece of music had been stolen that very evening from the attic. As the three girls were preparing for bed, Nancy told her chums about smelling the smoke up there. Then she asked:

''Did you see the paper in the hand of the man we were chasing?''

The girls nodded. ''You think it was a sheet of music?''

"I'm afraid so. There's no telling how long thieving may have been going on here. For years, perhaps. And there'd be no way to trace it. Well, if I can't locate the music, perhaps I can at least find a clue to the thief right in this house.''

"How?"

"I have an idea. We'll try it out in the morning,'' said Nancy.

CHAPTER XVI

A Secret Drawer

Pressed by her chums for an explanation, Nancy revealed her suspicions that there might be a secret entrance to the attic.

"When that man left the grounds he had a roll of paper under his arm," she said. "He didn't have it when I saw him sneak toward the house."

"And you think he got it out of the attic?" questioned Bess.

"I'm convinced of it. Grandfather March and I both heard the floor up there creak, and I know someone was smoking."

As soon as Effie arrived in the morning to take over the housekeeping duties, Nancy and her friends went outdoors to examine the old mansion for signs of a secret entrance.

"How do we go about looking for such a thing?" asked Bess.

"Hunt for clapboards that can be moved," replied Nancy. "Secret doors alongside real ones, false windows, hidden——"

"That's enough to start with," laughed George.

The girls separated. For an hour they inspected every inch of the foundation and first floor walls. Nancy spent a long time in the old slave quarters to see if there might be any kind of an opening into the main part of the house. Failure met all their efforts.

"The man must have wings," sighed George.

"Maybe he comes down the chimney like Santa Claus," Bess giggled.

"There's only one thing left for us to do," said Nancy. "Hide in the bushes tonight and spy on the intruder."

"Before that happens, what do we do? Get some sleep?" asked George.

"I propose we go up to the attic and hunt for a secret entrance," suggested Nancy.

The three friends trooped to the third floor.

"I once heard knocking sounds up here," said Nancy. "Maybe there's a secret panel somewhere that has to be tapped on in order to open it."

As she began rapping her knuckles against the low walls under the sloping roof, Bess's feeling of spookiness returned.

"Nancy, do be careful. You may step on something like a hidden spring in the floor and just drop out of sight," she cautioned tremulously.

"Thanks, Bess, I will be careful."

True to her word, Nancy moved with the greatest caution. Bess insisted upon holding onto her friend's shoulder so that she could rescue her in case of an accident.

George in the meantime was looking through

an old bureau. Remembering that Mr. March's bank account needed substantial additions to keep him and Susan from applying for charity, the girl kept her eyes open for saleable articles.

"Here's some beautiful lace," she called out, taking it from the drawer.

"Let me see that!" cried Bess.

George held up several of the dainty pieces.

"Old lace is valuable," declared Bess, going across the attic to examine them. "Oh," she sighed, "we girls should wear more lace. In olden times ladies appreciated its lure! The great ladies of the Court knew its power!"

"Yes," said George with a grimace. "You know who first thought of lace, don't you? Fishermen. The first lace was a fish net, made to lure food from the sea!"

"George, you're disgustingly unromantic," said her cousin. "Someone who appreciates beautiful things will pay Mr. March a good price for this lovely work."

"Have you anyone in mind?"

"Yes. The dressmaker, Madame Paray."

"Maybe she'll put some of it on a dress for Diane Dight," grinned George.

Nancy gave a start at this remark. For several hours she had forgotten all about the Dight family. Now she recalled in full force her unpleasant experiences with them. She had not forgotten the shock she had received over the letter Diane had been reading the morning she had called at the house.

"It certainly is a mystery to me how she can be involved with——"

At that instant Bess screamed, "Oh! Take it away!"

Nancy and George sprang toward the girl. The skeleton had its hand in her hair!

"Take it away! Hurry!"

Bess stood as if transfixed. She had backed up toward the wardrobe, and the door had opened suddenly. The long, bony fingers had reached out and enmeshed themselves in her hair.

Quickly Nancy released its hold. Bess sank shaking upon a trunk.

"Oh, I don't like this attic," she said tremulously. "The way that—that skeleton looks at me, I feel as if some terrible tragedy has taken place up here."

"I told you the skeleton was brought here by a medical student," Nancy chided her.

"Then maybe the tragedy is about to happen!"

"Bess, I'm ashamed of you," her cousin George scolded. "Where's your courage?"

The other girl, still upset, could not throw off her mood of fear.

"See the way that skeleton hangs there with one bony arm half upraised?" Bess pointed out. "Just as if it were beckoning to us to come into the closet!"

"Why, so it does!" agreed Nancy. She moved closer to the wardrobe. "You know, you may have hit upon the solution to a great many things.''

"Close the door!" pleaded Bess. "Don't you dare step inside!"

Nancy paid no attention to her. Thinking aloud, she remarked, "Perhaps Fipp March placed the skeleton that way to convey a message to his family. Possibly there's a secret hiding place——"

"Oh, Nancy, do close the door!" urged Bess again.

While she looked on with disapproval, Nancy began an examination of the massive wardrobe. She had done this before, but this time she paid particular attention to the section underneath the skeleton. Inch by inch she ran her hand over the floor of the big piece of furniture.

"Hold the flashlight, will you, George?" she asked.

Obediently the other girl came closer.

"I can feel something with my fingers!" Nancy said in an excited voice. "A little bump in the wood!"

"Probably it's a knothole," George contributed skeptically.

"It's a tiny knob!" corrected Nancy. "Girls, I've found a secret compartment!"

Again and again she tugged, trying to open it. The wood had swollen from dampness and the lid was stuck fast.

"Let me try my luck!" urged George impatiently.

Before George could test her strength, Effie appeared at the head of the stairs.

"Miss Nancy, there's a man downstairs to see you," she announced.

"To see me? I didn't think anyone knew I was here."

"Mrs. Gruen sent him," explained Effie. "And he says he can't wait long."

"What's his name?"

"Mr. Jenner."

The publisher of Ben Banks' music!

CHAPTER XVII

An Unpleasant Caller

The unexpected call from the music publisher surprised Nancy. She asked Bess and George if they wanted to continue working on the secret space in the cabinet, or go downstairs with her.

"Maybe we can find some evidence against Mr. Jenner while you're talking to him," George suggested. "This—lid—ought to open pretty soon," she added, tugging at the knob in the floor of the wardrobe.

Nancy hurried down the stairs to meet the song publisher. She was sorry that Mr. March had gone to town and could not see Mr. Jenner.

"But perhaps it's just as well that he isn't here," she reasoned. "The poor man gets so excited thinking of his son's music having been stolen that he might say something to harm his own chances."

Mr. Jenner proved to be an unpleasant-looking man with a calculating face and a brisk manner.

"I've not much time to spend here," he said snappily. "My time is very limited. Are you Miss Nancy Drew?"

"I am," replied the girl calmly.

Mr. Jenner did not waste words. He spoke of the communications which she had sent to him. "Although you didn't say anything definite, you hinted at an accusation."

"Did my note give you that impression?" Nancy inquired coolly. She did not like this man.

"It certainly did, Miss Drew. First you asked me to give you Mr. Ben Banks' address. Then you mentioned wanting to discuss a matter of great importance with me."

"What do you know of Mr. Banks?"

"Very little. Most of our contact has been through correspondence."

"What can you tell me about a composer named Harry Hall?"

"He is another of my song writers—a very talented person. I've never met him, for he always sends his work in by mail."

"Can you vouch for his honesty?"

"What is this, a quiz program?" the publisher demanded, getting red in the face. "I'll admit I don't know much about either of the men, but their music is equal to the best that is being put out today."

"And for good reason, perhaps," smiled Nancy.

"What do you mean? Don't tell me you think someone else wrote it!"

"Perhaps you should make sure no one else did," replied the girl, "before you publish it."

"Will you tell me who has been making such inferences?" snapped the man.

"No one," Nancy replied. "I thought I would give you an opportunity to explain what you know about the matter."

"I've nothing to explain! I publish the music in good faith. I'm satisfied that the men with whom I deal are the true composers of the songs they submit to me."

"And are you prepared to prove it?"

"Certainly I am," Mr. Jenner returned wrathfully. He glanced at his watch. "I made a special trip here to see you, and my valuable time has been wasted."

"You may not think so later."

"What are your reasons for believing that Banks and Hall are plagiarists?"

"I can't tell you at this moment," responded Nancy. "I do suggest that you buy no more music from either of those men until the matter of the rightful composer has been straightened out."

"Who is the mysterious person you claim wrote the music?"

"I can't tell you."

"Well, it doesn't worry me in the least," retorted the publisher. "I'll admit I was a little disturbed when I received your letter today. But now that I've met you, I realize you're only an irresponsible schoolgirl. Stupid of me to waste so much time coming here."

Without so much as a good-by, Mr. Jenner left the house. With mingled feelings of annoyance and contempt, Nancy watched the music publisher drive away. She was afraid that perhaps she had revealed too much. She would have been greatly disturbed had she known that Mr. Jenner was heading for the hotel where Ben Banks lived.

"Has your caller left so soon?" questioned Bess, when Nancy returned to the attic. "We haven't opened the secret compartment yet."

"When we do, I hope it will contain something I can use against Mr. Jenner," said Nancy, and went on to tell her friends of the man's remarks.

Bess and George were incensed. "All I can say is that if Nancy Drew, Detective, once gets on his trail, he'd better look out!" George exclaimed, her eyes blazing.

"Well, after all, I do need evidence," sighed Nancy. "Come on, let's get at this lid again."

Nancy gave the knob a quick jerk sideways. A little door pulled up, revealing a recess below.

"It's open!" cried Nancy in delight. "Let's hope Fipp's songs are here!"

Eagerly she thrust her hand into the hole.

"Papers!" she exclaimed.

Quickly she pulled out a handful. It was difficult to look at them by her flashlight, so the girls took everything out of the drawer and carried the contents to one of the bedrooms.

Grandfather March had come in and now eagerly helped to look through the mass of old letters and papers.

"There's no music here," Bess said in disappointment a few minutes later. "Only a few letters."

"They're in the handwriting of Fipp's old nurse Ada!" observed Mr. March. Snatching one of the yellowed sheets, he read it eagerly.

"This was written to Fipp when he was in college! I've never seen these letters before."

One by one the elderly man looked through the communications, reading some of them aloud. Suddenly Nancy uttered a pleased exclamation.

"Here's a clue! Please read that again!"

Grandfather March adjusted his glasses and re-read the letter.

> Dear Fipp,
> The melody you say has haunted you since Thanksgiving Day runs as follows: (An eight bar melody was sketched.)
> It is a lovely tune which your dear, deceased mother often hummed. I remember well when she composed it.

"Don't you see?" cried Nancy. "The nurse Ada is sort of a witness for you, Mr. March. If your son wrote a song elaborating on this melody, and you find Ben Banks claims to be the composer, you'll have some proof against him!"

"I admit I don't recall this particular melody," Mr. March confessed. "If Fipp used it, he probably did so when he was away from home."

Bess and George had been sorting the papers which were not letters. Now they cried out simultaneously:

"Here's a piece of original music! It says 'By Fipp March. Based on a melody composed by his mother.' "

Eagerly the group stared at the double sheet. Tears came to Grandfather March's eyes. Then he smiled.

"Those thieves didn't get this, thank goodness. I'd like to hear it. Will you play it, Nancy?"

Everyone went downstairs to the music room. Nancy did the best she could on the old piano, while Bess and George hummed the melody.

"It's lovely," said Bess dreamily.

"It would be a song hit if it were published," declared George.

"My father knows a reputable music publisher," said Nancy. "Maybe he would buy it."

"Take it home with you," Mr. March urged, "and send it to him."

At home half an hour later, Nancy played the selection for her father and Mrs. Gruen on her own piano. Both shared her enthusiasm for the lovely music, and declared that it was the equal of the best popular songs on the market.

"I can't make rash promises, but I believe

Mr. Hawkins will buy the song,'' Mr. Drew said to his daughter. ''I'll write to him tonight. He's a good friend of mine and a client as well, and we may get some excellent results.''

Satisfied that her father would do what he could for Mr. March, Nancy now told him of her plan to try to capture the intruder at Pleasant Hedges.

''I feel sure he's getting in by some secret entrance. But I can't locate it. So tonight I plan to watch if possible.''

''Promise me you won't do it unless Bess and George are with you.''

''All right, Dad. And now tell me about the Booker case. Has the chemical fluid I brought been analyzed yet?'' Nancy asked.

''Mr. Booker is having his chief chemist examine the solution and compare it with preparations used in his own plant. So far I've received no report.''

''I wish they'd hurry,'' said Nancy impatiently.

''If you want some action, why not see Mr. Dight again?'' her father teased her. ''He can't be too pleased about the way you disappeared while in his factory.''

Nancy made a grimace. ''Do you think he found out I was there?''

''Mr. Dight is thorough in his methods. I shouldn't be surprised if he's called in several experts to take fingerprints and solve the riddle of the light you turned on in the laboratory.''

"Fingerprints!" gasped Nancy. "I never once thought of that angle. Why, I left them everywhere—in the laboratory, in the spidery, even the tunnel!"

"Then I advise you to steer clear of Mr. Dight unless you're looking for trouble."

"That's just it," Nancy replied with a little moan. "I'll have to see him. Mr. Dight still has those valuable old bottles belonging to Grandfather March. If I don't go back for them, he'll be doubly suspicious. He may even move all the evidence before you can prosecute him."

The more Nancy thought of interviewing Mr. Dight, the more she dreaded it. On second thought, she doubted the man had looked for fingerprints, though there still was no telling what he had found out. Nevertheless, late that afternoon she drove to the factory grounds. With no outward display of nervousness, she greeted Miss Jones, the private secretary.

"May I see Mr. Dight, please?" she requested.

The secretary, formerly so friendly, gazed at her without smiling.

"Yes, Mr. Dight very much wants to talk to you, Miss Drew," she replied with emphasis.

CHAPTER XVIII

WATCHING

NANCY's heart sank, but she realized she must play a part if she expected to keep out of trouble.

"Your sudden disappearance from Mr. Dight's office the other day disturbed him very much," Miss Jones continued.

Nancy pretended not to understand. "My disappearance? Why, didn't Mr. Dight think that when I left his office I was going home?"

"Apparently he didn't. He thought you went off somewhere in the factory."

"Well, no wonder you were worried!"

"I'll tell Mr. Dight you are here," the young woman said, rising.

In a moment she returned to say that Nancy might enter the man's private office. The factory owner sat at his desk, writing. For several seconds he kept on, paying no attention to his young visitor. Finally he looked up.

"Well?" he barked, trying to place the girl on the defensive. "Did you learn what you were sent here for?"

Nancy knew that Mr. Dight suspected she had

148

been assigned by someone, perhaps her father, to spy on him, but she pretended otherwise.

"Oh, you mean about the bottles?" she said brightly. "I'm sorry I ran off the way I did, but I saw someone in the courtyard I thought I knew. Then it was so late I decided to go on home."

Mr. Dight gazed quizzically at Nancy.

"And did you go directly home from here?" he questioned her sharply.

Nancy was not to be trapped so easily. "Well, you know how it is," she laughed. "I didn't mean to worry anyone, but I have many friends. I'll confess I didn't get home until rather late. Our housekeeper was quite upset."

"I can imagine," replied Mr. Dight.

The man had been completely won over by Nancy. He decided that the light in the laboratory must have turned on because of some vibration in the place. Bushy Trott had found nothing out of order. He had not even seen the black widow which Nancy had killed.

Leaning back in his swivel chair, Mr. Dight suddenly relaxed. In a friendly tone he began to discuss Mr. March's collection of bottles. "I've taken quite a fancy to some of that glassware. Now, if you'll name your price, young lady, perhaps we can do business."

"The blue bottle was intended as a gift."

"I'll buy the others. Suppose I offer you thirty-five dollars for the entire collection?"

Nancy's face fell. She had expected Mr.

Dight to make a low offer, but certainly not one under a hundred dollars.

"Only thirty-five?" she asked in a weak voice. "Oh, I couldn't sell them for that."

"I might make it fifty," Mr. Dight bargained. "You're a friend of Diane's, so I'll throw in the extra fifteen for good measure."

Nancy arose, glad of an excuse to withdraw in good grace.

"I couldn't think of letting friendship influence me in this transaction," she assured the factory owner, "because I'm selling the bottles for someone else. I don't believe the person would be willing to part with them for thirty-five dollars."

"I'll pay you fifty, but not a cent more."

"I'll find out if that's satisfactory," Nancy said, standing firm. She had already decided to consult the antique dealer, Mr. Faber, on the subject. "May I have the bottles, please?"

Obviously unwilling to let the fine collection out of his possession, Mr. Dight raised his price another ten dollars. When Nancy would not sell them, he reluctantly returned the box of glassware to her.

Nancy gave a sigh of relief as she got into her car. She hoped never to have to face Mr. Dight again!

She drove directly to Mr. Faber's shop, and carried her box into the quaint little place. The pleasant owner, who spoke with a slight accent, greeted her as an old friend.

"Well, well, and what have you brought me this time? Not one of Madame Alexandra's jewels to sell?"

"Oh, no," laughed Nancy. "Since Madame has had no more people troubling her, she's had no reason to dispose of her Court treasures."

"Thanks to you," said Mr. Faber, bowing. "Madame owes you a great debt, as do I. Pray, how may I serve you?"

"I have some bottles I'd like to have you look at."

Nancy spread them over a counter already cluttered with odds and ends of beautiful things from every corner of the world. Mr. Faber's blue eyes began to sparkle.

"These bottles are old and fine!" he exclaimed, appraising them at a glance. "I will pay you a very good price for them."

"Friendship mustn't enter into this," cautioned Nancy. "Tell me frankly, are the bottles worth fifty dollars?"

"I will pay you double that amount gladly! If you are in no great hurry for the money, perhaps I can sell them to a collector who will pay an even higher price."

"The bottles are yours to do with as you wish," Nancy decided instantly. "Perhaps, though, you'd better write a check for a hundred dollars now to Mr. Philip March. Let me know if there'll be more later."

"Always you are busy helping someone," Mr. Faber beamed at the girl, as he handed her the check. "Is it not so? And that fine young man who assisted you in settling Madame Alexandra's affairs so nicely! A handsome pair you made together, but of late I have not seen him."

"Ned's been pretty busy," Nancy replied. Not wishing to answer any personal questions, she edged toward the door. "Well, I'll have to run along."

At home Nancy found a telegram awaiting her. It was from Mr. Jenner, the music publisher.

The message both disappointed and annoyed her. Curtly the man informed her that she had made a great mistake in assuming the songs he had published had been stolen.

"Any further accusations by you will lead to a libel suit," he warned her. "Advise you pursue matter no further. Otherwise expect us to take immediate action against you."

Nancy was not fooled by the threat.

"He is frightened and is just trying to scare me," she thought. "Mr. Jenner and Ben Banks must be closely associated."

While wondering what her next move should be, Nancy walked out onto the porch and sat down on a rattan lounge. Suddenly someone sat down in the chair beside her.

Horace Lally!

"Hello, Attractive," he said familiarly. "You look sort of worried. What's on your mind?"

"Nothing," replied Nancy. "Nothing at all; nor in it, for that matter."

"Oh, come now, you're too modest," bantered Horace. "I'll bet a cent you're worrying about what you'll wear to the dance."

"Please, Horace, I said I wasn't going."

"Bess and George gave me to understand you'd change your mind," he said, looking hurt. "And you're the one person I want to be there when the important announcement is made."

"Can't you tell me what it is?"

"I'll give you a hint. It concerns a very good friend of yours, and will startle the professional world."

Despite herself, Nancy was curious to learn more. Still, she did not care to go to the dance with Horace.

At that moment Helen Corning chanced to come down the street. The two girls were close friends, and Nancy called her to the porch. Immediately Horace appealed to her to talk Nancy into going to Emerson with him.

Helen was surprised that apparently Ned Nickerson had not asked her friend. But she saw no reason because of this for Nancy to stay home.

"Of course you ought to go!" she said. "Why, you've never missed a college dance!"

Nancy was in a tight spot. Bess, George, and now Helen, were all on Horace's side.

"Horace, please ask someone else," she begged.

"It's getting pretty late now."

"Oh, you still have a few days. But I tell you, if you really can't find anyone, let me know. I'll see then what I'll do."

The minute he had gone, Nancy was provoked at herself for having given even a halfway promise. Furthermore, she was very embarrassed when Helen inquired about Ned. Nancy was glad that her friend left so soon.

Bess and George had decided to go back to Pleasant Hedges for the night, so the three girls drove out there after an early supper. They found Mr. March following his usual custom of relating stories to his little grandchild.

"There are some war stories I can't tell her," he said, greeting them, "but maybe you'd like to hear them some time."

When he and the girls had gone downstairs, he pulled a little book from his pocket.

"It's because of this that I'm alive today," he said. "Bullets were flying thick and fast. One of them had my name on it, but it didn't get me!"

"What do you mean, had your name on it?" asked Bess.

"Well, that's a figure of speech, of course. This bullet struck me, but I never knew it, for it embedded itself in this little book."

Grandfather March showed them a battered, leather-covered diary bearing an ugly hole.

"It gives me the chills," said Bess. "How fortunate you were!"

"How I wish Susan's father might have been as lucky," sighed the elderly soldier. "But he has left us something fine. We must not let anyone take it from us."

Nancy told him of her plan to watch the house that evening, hoping to catch the mysterious intruder.

"We're going to lie in wait for him outdoors this time," she explained.

Mr. March was concerned. "I don't know that I should let you do this," he said. "It's risky, and may not be worth the price."

"Three of us girls ought to be able to handle one man!" boasted George.

Nancy assured the owner of Pleasant Hedges that they would take no unnecessary chances. She had suggested that the three of them wear dark dresses and cover their hair with black kerchiefs. Now as they left the house and stealthily took their separate posts which Nancy had assigned to them, they seemed like weird, mysterious shadows.

Within the house, life went on in the usual routine way. Susan was put to bed. Effie cleared away the supper and went upstairs. Grandfather March seated himself in the dining room to listen to the radio for clues to any songs stolen from his son. Finally he turned off the radio, put out the light, and climbed the stairs to the second floor.

Nancy and the other girls shifted their positions in the darkness outside. There had been no sign of a trespasser. An owl hooted dismally, making Bess shiver.

"I've been here three hours already," she thought. "And it's a long time until sunrise."

It had been decided that if no one appeared by that time, the chances were nobody would. Then the three girls were to meet and give up the watch.

From somewhere in the old mansion a clock began to strike, weird and deep in the stillness of the night. Nancy, posted near the slave quarters, counted eleven.

Suddenly from a distance there came sounds of something stirring. Nancy stood erect, listening intently.

She was puzzled. One moment she thought she could hear a soft pad, as if someone were sneaking among the pine trees toward the house. The next minute she was sure light footsteps were approaching from the front of the mansion.

"Maybe the thief has an accomplice," she told herself.

There was no doubt of it. Two figures were coming nearer and nearer. Nancy held her breath!

CHAPTER XIX

Under the Wallpaper

As Nancy waited, the two shadowy forms crept closer. The one coming across the lawn appeared first. All of a sudden the voice of the other cut the air like a shot from a pistol.

"Nancy, where are you?"

Grandfather March!

His ill-timed call served as a warning to the other man. Instantly the stranger turned and fled.

Nancy dashed from her hiding place. As she pursued the running figure, she shouted to her friends to join in the chase.

They came quickly, but the race was futile. The night swallowed up the intruder. As the discouraged girls returned to the house, Nancy explained what had happened. George was annoyed.

"It's bad enough to have missed capturing the thief, but now he has been warned that we're looking for him," she declared.

"We've probably missed our chance, too, of finding out how he gets into the house," added Nancy in disappointment.

"Oh, why did Mr. March have to pick out

157

just that moment to look for us?'' complained Bess.

"I suppose he meant well," said Nancy.

The elderly soldier was apologetic at his sudden appearance. He had become uneasy about the girls, he explained, and had come outside to make sure they were all right. When no one spoke to him, he had grown afraid something had happened to them, and had called out, unaware of the nearness of the intruder.

It was decided that the mysterious stranger certainly would not return that night, so the girls went to bed, Nancy sharing a big old-fashioned four-poster with her chums. Upon awakening the next morning, she heard faint strains of music from a distance.

"Mr. March has the radio on early," she thought.

When Nancy reached the dining room, she found him and Susan already at the breakfast table. But neither of them was eating. They were listening to a man singing.

"One of my Daddy's pieces, Nancy!" cried the little girl.

"Sh!" her grandfather said, putting a finger to his lips.

As Nancy listened, she realized this composition was somewhat different from the others Mr. March attributed to his son. It was a beautiful love song in waltz time. Three words caught the girl's attention. "My heart's desire——"

"Where have I heard that phrase before in connection with this mystery?" she mused.

For nearly an hour the melody continued to haunt her. Then suddenly she knew why. Running to Mr. March, she exclaimed:

"I believe you were right in the first place about the clue to the missing music."

"How's that?"

"Why, those love letters written by your son to his wife! The words, 'My Heart's Desire,' appear in one of them!"

"So they do," the elderly man agreed musingly.

Nancy was eager to read the love notes again. Since they were still at her own home, she decided to leave Pleasant Hedges at once and go there. But her plans were changed by Susan and a game the child wanted to play, the outcome of which was to have startling consequences.

"Please dress up with me," the little girl begged. "Effie showed me some long dresses —funny old ones. Let's put them on."

To humor the child, Nancy agreed to play for half an hour.

"Come upstairs and I'll show you what you're to wear!" commanded Susan, tugging at Nancy's hand.

A closet yielded a strange assortment of old-fashioned garments. Susan presented Nancy with a lavender silk gown having a pinched waist and many ruffles. For herself she chose a flowered crepe dress with a bustle. Holding up the trailing skirt with one hand, she flourished a silk parasol in the other.

"Let's go down and show Grandpa how we look," Susan insisted. "Do I look like a real grown-up lady now?"

"Those high-heeled shoes certainly make you seem taller," Nancy smiled. "Watch out, or you'll trip!"

The words were hardly out of her mouth when the child stumbled. She had started down the steps, swinging the parasol jauntily. Now her foot caught in the long, flowing skirt she wore.

Nancy made a grab for Susan and reached her just in time. But the sharp-pointed parasol got out of control and tore a jagged hole in the wallpaper.

"Oh, I didn't mean to do it!" Susan cried in dismay. "What will Grandpa say?"

"It wasn't your fault," replied Nancy kindly. "Fortunately, you weren't hurt. Let's see if the paper can be pasted back on again."

She came down the steps to examine the torn place. The girl scarcely could believe her eyes. Several tiny bars of music were painted on the wall! Nancy summoned Grandfather March to the stairway. At first he thought she was calling attention to the costumes, but when he saw the notes before his eyes, he too became excited.

"Maybe the music is part of one of our old

family songs!" he exclaimed. "I'd like to know if there's any more of it here. Let's tear off the paper," urged Mr. March. "It's too faded to worry about anyway."

Inch by inch Mr. March, Nancy, Bess and George removed a large area of the wall covering. It was slow, tedious work, but at last they were successful. Gradually a charming, old-fashioned scene was revealed of a woman seated at a piano and a man beside her singing.

The last bit of paper to come off partially covered the music rack of the piano pictured on the painted scene. Someone with artistic ability had sketched in a sheet of music, the notes of which had first drawn Nancy's attention. In tiny lettering was printed the composer's name, a member of the March family.

"That's one of the melodies Fipp used. He must have picked it up while hearing his grandmother sing it," said Mr. March.

Nancy hummed the pictured notes. The simple tune was indeed one which had been elaborated upon.

"Now we have real proof that Ben Banks is an impostor! This is one of the melodies he claims as his!"

"Would a court accept such evidence?" asked George.

"I think it would," said Nancy soberly. "Of course, it might not be necessary to go to court about it. If Mr. Jenner knows we have a case against him, he probably will prefer to settle matters without a lawsuit. If you wish, Mr. March, I'll see the publisher.''

"Yes, do that,'' urged the elderly man. "You're right clever at handling folks.''

Nancy asked Bess and George if they would go with her to Oxford where Mr. Jenner's offices were located. The town was several miles from River Heights, and the trip would mean a tedious train ride. The girls were eager to go and suggested starting at once.

"I've always wanted to visit Tin Pan Alley,'' remarked Bess with a giggle, as they neared Oxford, "and meet a real composer.''

"Tin Pan Alley is in New York—not Oxford,'' returned George with a sniff. "And we're hunting for a plagiarist.''

The three girls made the journey from the station to 605 Bridewell Place by taxi. The street was a narrow one, rather dirty, and with buildings crowded close together.

"This isn't very inviting,'' said Nancy, gazing at the dingy brown brick structure that was their destination.

From an upstairs room came the halting strains of a swing band. In another section of the building someone was picking out a few notes on a piano.

Nancy led the way to the elevator, but found it was not in use. The girls climbed the stairs.

"Listen!'' bade Nancy suddenly.

"I don't hear anything except that loud music," declared George. "The tune is catchy, but all those discords!"

"It's one of Fipp March's songs!" insisted the Drew girl. "Whoever is playing it, isn't doing it very well, either!"

The girls moved nearer to the closed door. The piano playing ceased abruptly. After waiting a moment, they went along the hall until they came to a door which bore the name of the music publisher. Nancy and her friends entered.

They found themselves in an untidy little room. A desk was piled high with papers, books, and stacks of music. An office girl with frowsy hair sat at a typewriter. She chewed gum to the rhythm of her typing and did not look up for a long while.

"Well?" she inquired at last.

"May we see Mr. Jenner, please?" requested Nancy politely.

The girl looked her over from head to toe.

"If you have music to sell, you've come to the wrong place. Mr. Jenner ain't buying from amateurs."

"I have nothing to sell," replied Nancy with dignity. "Please give my name to your employer."

She removed a card from her purse. The office girl accepted it with a shrug and vanished into an inner room. She did not return for several minutes. Then her message was crisp and to the point.

"Toddle along," she said rudely. "Mr. Jenner ain't seeing you."

"But I've come all the way from River Heights——"

"Mr. Jenner ain't seeing nobody today," the girl interrupted. "Only one of his composers. And he said to tell you it wouldn't do no good to come back later either!"

"I see," said Nancy.

Flushing slightly, she turned away.

"I was afraid this might happen," she declared, as the girls paused in the hall.

"We've made this trip for nothing," said Bess. "It's a shame."

"I feel like going back in there and demanding an interview!" said Nancy.

"You can't do that," George replied, taking her chum by the arm. "Come along."

"Let your father handle that horrid man," suggested Bess.

Determined not to go home without finding out something, Nancy paused again. Then she walked down the corridor where she suspected Mr. Jenner's private office was located. Through an open transom came voices.

"Ben, we're in a tight spot," they heard the music publisher say. "That Drew girl has just left here. Maybe she *has* found some proof."

"Impossible!" replied the other voice.

"Just the same, it may be well to call off the Emerson College performance. We can't take chances."

Nancy and her chums strained their ears to

hear more. However, the voices dropped and the girls could not make out another word.

"Mr. Jenner must be talking to Ben Banks!" Nancy whispered excitedly. "Oh, I wish we could learn more about that fellow!"

"Maybe we can," said George in her friend's ear. "Why not stay around here until he comes out of the office?"

"And then follow him!" added Nancy. "You girls wait outside the building. I'll watch this door."

Bess and George immediately tiptoed down the hallway and vanished. Nancy looked about for a hiding place. The best one she could find was a little niche near the old elevator shaft.

Twenty minutes elapsed. At the end of that time the door of Mr. Jenner's office swung open. Out stepped a lean, long-haired man of early middle age. He had a roll of music under his arm. Nancy was convinced that he must be Ben Banks.

Waiting until he had rounded the corner, she followed him downstairs. At the street level she spied Bess and George standing in a shadowy doorway. With a nod of her head she signaled to them.

The two girls immediately started off in pursuit of Ben Banks. Nancy waited until she was certain her movements would not arouse the song writer's attention or suspicion. Then she hastened after her chums and caught up with them.

The man walked rapidly. Of one thing

Nancy was certain. He was not the strange intruder at the March homestead. That fellow was heavy-set.

Without once glancing back, Banks kept on until he came to a small hotel, the Milette. Entering, he went directly to the desk.

Nancy, Bess, and George stood in the lobby. They heard the man say to the desk clerk:

"My key, please."

"Yes, Mr. Lally," the other replied, handing it to him.

"Lally!" Nancy almost exclaimed aloud.

CHAPTER XX

A MEAN MIX-UP

NANCY and her chums wondered if they had heard correctly. The name of the man they thought was Ben Banks was Lally! To make sure of this, the girls waited until the man had gone up in the elevator. Then they went to the desk.

"Is Mr. Banks registered here?" Nancy asked, smiling at the clerk.

"You mean the composer? Yes, but he uses his own name of Lally. I'm sorry, but Mr. Lally cannot see you now. Someone is waiting for him in his room."

The girls left the hotel. On the way to the train and during the ride back to River Heights, they discussed the matter from all angles.

"Do you suppose Mr. Lally can be related to Horace?" asked Bess.

"We heard Mr. Jenner mention Emerson College," George replied. "And Horace hinted to you, Nancy, about some sort of mysterious announcement. Possibly it's about music."

"This so-called Ben Banks may be a relative of Horace," Nancy agreed thoughtfully. "I shall make it my business to find out. If he is, what a tangle this mystery is getting into!"

In the light of the day's discovery, the Emerson dance took on new significance. At home once more, Nancy began to wonder if Horace would press his invitation again. She had not been in the house fifteen minutes when the dreaded call came. Horace, as always, was very sure of himself.

"Well, Nancy," he said breezily. "You can start planning on what you'll wear Saturday night. I'll meet you at the Emerson station on the five o'clock train."

"Just a minute," said the girl. "I haven't said I'd go with you."

"You promised you'd come if I couldn't get another girl. Well, I didn't!"

Nancy was dismayed but tried to hide her confusion. Without offering any reply, she switched the subject and asked Horace if he had a relative who composed music.

"Sure," the boy answered, suspecting nothing. "My Uncle Ben does. And I do too! You ought to hear some of my songs—hot stuff! You'll learn all about them at the dance."

"What do you mean, Horace?"

"Oh, I shouldn't have told you," the youth checked himself. "It's part of the surprise. Don't tell anyone, will you? We'll go early and——"

The connection suddenly was broken.

Nancy sagged weakly in her chair. Horace Lally a nephew of Ben Lally, alias Ben Banks, the plagiarist!

"And the worst of it is, I've virtually promised to go to the dance with Horace," she thought in horror. "Why, I'm like a fly walking right into a spider's web—with my eyes open!"

The telephone rang again. Nancy was tempted not to answer it. She felt certain Horace was calling a second time. He would demand a definite answer to his invitation. She did not know what to tell him.

"Oh, well, I can't evade the question any longer," she thought. "I'll have to make up my mind."

With a sinking heart, she reached for the receiver. To Nancy's relief, it was not Horace Lally who telephoned, but Bess Marvin. The girl's voice quivered with excitement.

"Nancy, I just heard—" she began.

"Yes?"

"From a boy at Emerson——"

"What about?" asked Nancy.

"Why, the dance. Ned Nickerson is taking Diane Dight!"

Nancy did not speak for a moment. The news came as a distinct shock to her. Ned, of course, had a right to invite any girl he might choose. But of all persons, why had he asked Diane?

"He doesn't know that her father is on the verge of being hailed into court as a thief," she reflected. "I can't tell Ned that either. The information must be kept secret."

Matters were hourly getting into a worse

tangle. As soon as Mr. Drew came in, Nancy asked him how things stood in the Dight case.

"Not good for him. Mr. Booker has just informed me that his chemist has analyzed the bottles of fluid you obtained from the Dight factory."

"With what result, Dad?"

"The solutions are the same as those used in the Booker plant to toughen the spider thread."

"Then Mr. Dight did steal the formula—or rather, hired Bushy Trott to do it!"

"It appears that way, Nancy. I've decided to prosecute Dight as soon as I can prepare my case against him."

Nancy told her father about Ned having asked Diane to the dance, and of her wish to keep the young man out of any unpleasant publicity connected with the Dight family.

Mr. Drew lapsed into silence for a few moments. Then he smiled at his daughter.

"Ned hardly deserves such thoughtfulness on your part," he said. "But I see your side of it. Of course, you can't reveal anything to him. I tell you how we'll solve that problem! I'll hold up the proceedings against Mr. Dight until the dance is over."

Nancy thanked her father. Then she went on to tell him what she had learned about Ben Banks. Mr. Drew raised his eyebrows when he heard that the man was the uncle of Horace Lally.

"Affairs *are* getting in a muddle," the lawyer agreed.

"I certainly need your advice," Nancy said.

"Do you want to go to the dance with Horace? If so, we can wait before bringing action against his uncle."

"Aren't you forgetting one detail?"

"What's that?"

"Ben Banks learned from Mr. Jenner that a certain Nancy Drew knows something about him. It's natural that he'll mention my name to Horace."

"I never thought of that angle!" exclaimed Mr. Drew. "You're right, Nancy."

"Then what am I to do? Horace doesn't know the truth yet. He keeps telephoning me, demanding an answer, and unfortunately I half promised to go with him."

"I don't see anything for you to do but to leave home for a while!"

"I'll do it! The March mansion will serve my purpose," said Nancy enthusiastically. "There's a lot there I want to do. Dad, you're a life saver!"

"Have you found any more music?"

Nancy shook her head.

"Better do so. Mr. Hawkins has bought that song of Fipp March's you brought me."

"Really!" exclaimed Nancy joyfully.

"The letter came this morning from the publisher. He liked the song very much, and he wants more of the same kind of music."

"If only I could supply it! So far I've not been able to find another piece, Dad. But I believe I have a good clue this time."

She told her father about hearing a song on the radio which Mr. March believed to be one of Fipp's and which contained the phrase, "My heart's desire."

"I recall reading those words in one of the letters of young Mr. March to his wife Connie," Nancy explained. "I believe the clue to the missing music—if there's any that hasn't been stolen—may be in those letters after all. Suppose I get them——"

"You'd better pack some clothes and slip away from here," her father advised her, "or some of those complications you're trying to avoid will start happening."

"You're right. I'll leave at once and take the letters with me."

Nancy went upstairs to pack an overnight bag. As she gathered together a few toilet articles, Ned's smiling photograph stared at her from the dresser.

"Well, old friend," she whispered to it, a catch in her throat, "I hope your name won't be involved in anything unpleasant. You're too nice for that!"

Nancy did not put the picture in a drawer as she felt tempted to do. Instead, she completed her packing and then picked up the March love letters which she inadvertently had laid beside the photograph. Then she went downstairs.

Nancy was sorry to leave her father so soon, but he wanted her to get back to Pleasant Hedges while it was still daylight. She had had so much to talk to him about that she had forgotten completely to tell him of the appearance of the strange intruder at the old homestead. If she had, he would not have kissed her good-by so cheerily.

"I'll instruct Hannah not to let anyone know where you are," he said. "She can tell your friends that you'll be back in a few days."

Upon reaching the old mansion, Nancy immediately sought out Mr. March, and told him that Mr. Hawkins, her father's client, had bought Fipp's song.

"Oh, that's fine," said the elderly man, tears glistening in his eyes. "Now my son and the March family will have recognition at last. Nancy Drew, I never can repay you for what you've done!"

"Mr. Hawkins would like more songs," Nancy smiled. "I'm going to search harder than ever for them now. Here are your son's letters. Let's look through them for clues."

For some time the elderly man and his guest read without saying a word. Then suddenly Nancy cried out:

"Here's what I was looking for! Listen to this!"

CHAPTER XXI

Clues in Verse

NANCY read eagerly from one of Fipp March's letters to his wife.

No love more true than mine,
I would protect thee every day.
Among old things and fine,
I put my heart's desire away.

"It's a pretty verse," said Grandfather March. "But as to its being a clue——"

Nancy gave her interpretation of the words. "Your son wanted to provide for his wife always. He put the song with the words 'My Heart's Desire' among some fine old things. She was to find it and sell it if the need arose."

"I see. And you think he meant he hid it somewhere here in the attic?"

"Perhaps," the girl replied. "Let's see if we can find another clue among these letters."

In a very few minutes Nancy came across a lovely verse. "I believe I have found it!" she exclaimed excitedly, and read:

Long forgotten man,
My secret you hide,

174

Reveal it to my love,
That comfort may abide.

"That means less to me than the other verse," declared Mr. March. "What do you make of it?"

" 'Long forgotten man' must be the skeleton! He guards a secret which, when found, will bring comfort to your son's family!"

"Maybe," agreed the elderly man, "but you've already found the secret drawer in the wardrobe. There was only one song in it."

Nancy's enthusiasm was not to be dimmed. She insisted upon going to the attic at once to investigate the skeleton and its surroundings further. Mr. March followed her, carrying a flashlight.

"I can't stand many more disappointments," he said in a disheartened tone. "Each time I think something surely will come of the search, but only failures have been the result. I haven't enough money to start suit against Ben Banks, either."

"I have a hunch that this time we're going to be successful," Nancy tried to encourage him.

As soon as they reached the attic, she went to the old wardrobe.

"Be careful," Mr. March warned her. "I don't exactly trust that mysterious piece of furniture."

Nancy gingerly opened the door. This time she had a very different impression of the skeleton. It did not seem sinister to her; in fact, she could almost imagine it was trying to be friendly.

"Maybe that's just because we've met so often!" she thought with a smile. "Or else it holds a very vital clue to good fortune for Mr. March."

Carefully she removed the bony figure from the hook. Almost at once she noticed something which previously had escaped her attention. Where the skeleton's head had hung, a tiny hole could be seen on the back wall of the wardrobe!

"Perhaps this means something!" she said with increasing hope.

A small, round curtain rod lay on the floor. She picked it up and carefully ran one end through the circular hole in the wardrobe. The rod touched no wall or object beyond.

Puzzled, Nancy removed the rod and peered through the tiny hole. She could see nothing —not even a glimmer of light.

"That's odd," she said to Mr. March. "I always assumed that this wardrobe stood against an outside wall of the attic."

"I did myself," he said, mystified.

"There must be a room or niche beyond! Otherwise, we'd see daylight!" exclaimed Nancy.

Thrilled by the discovery, she said she would run downstairs and out-of-doors. When she inspected the exterior of the mansion critically, she could see that a small section of the main house connected with the roof over the slave quarters.

"There may be a secret room up there," she thought excitedly. "It certainly looks that way!"

Darting into the house, she hurried up to Grandfather March. Breathlessly, she told him of her discovery.

"I never knew of any hidden room!" he exclaimed. "But come to think of it, Fipp would disappear for hours at a time and we never knew where he was."

"Perhaps your son found a hidden room and kept it a secret for his music! Let's move the wardrobe."

They found it was too heavy for them to budge, so Nancy went off to summon Effie from her supper preparations.

"We want to move the wardrobe in the attic," Nancy said excitedly. "Will you please help us?"

"You mean give that skeleton a ride? Oh, Miss Nancy!"

The Drew girl laughed and said she was on the verge of an important discovery and needed assistance. Reluctantly Effie consented to help her.

"I'll have a side-ache for a week," she puffed, as they tugged at the old piece.

"Now what's wrong?" Nancy asked, when Effie stopped and stared in fear at something on the floor.

Effie pointed to a spider which scurried across the floor for refuge. Apparently it had crawled from behind the wardrobe.

"It's only a harmless one," Nancy told her. "Probably it came through the hole in the wall."

"Then there must be a lot of 'em in the room beyond! I'll bet that's where the black widow came from that poisoned me. Oh, don't go any farther!" she pleaded.

"Maybe Effie's right," said Grandfather March.

"We haven't seen a single poisonous spider since that first time," Nancy pointed out. "If there were any more, they would have come through. Let's see what's behind here."

By working together, the three finally succeeded in shifting the massive piece of furniture a few more inches. Susan, who had come upstairs, watched with deep interest. Suddenly she clapped her hands and began to dance.

"There it is! A door in the wall!"

"Sure's you're born, it is!" agreed Grandfather March, staring in astonishment.

The door was a crude, homemade affair, evidently built by a person little skilled in carpentry.

"Fipp must have put that in himself, the

rascal!" chuckled Grandfather March. "I'm sure it was not here when the house was built."

Nancy unbolted the door and pushed with all her strength. It refused to give.

"That's queer," said Grandfather March. "Let me try it."

He had no better success than Nancy.

"It must be bolted on the other side," the girl said.

Many thoughts flashed through her mind. The strange musical notes she had heard. The tapping sounds. They must have come from beyond this locked door. With no apparent opening to the place from the slave quarters, how did anyone get into the hidden spot? It almost seemed as if some supernatural creature might inhabit the mysterious abode.

As if the girl's thoughts were being read, Effie whispered hoarsely, "There's a ghost in there! Don't let it out!"

The remark brought Nancy down to earth. She was provoked that the maid had spoken, for her statement frightened Susan. The child clung to Nancy.

"Effie, go downstairs and take Susan with you," the Drew girl said rather severely. "There are no such things as ghosts and you know it. Mr. March and I will continue the work alone."

The maid, somewhat embarrassed, took the child downstairs. Although Nancy had declared there could not be a ghost beyond the locked door, she was apprehensive as to what they might find.

"Shall we break the door down?" she asked Mr. March.

The elderly soldier straightened his shoulders.

"I've never flinched yet in the face of danger," he said. "We came up here to find my son's music. If it lies beyond this door, I'm going to get it, no matter who or what I may face!"

Nancy was thrilled. Mr. March had expressed her own feelings!

Together they pushed against the door. Suddenly there was a splintering sound, and the whole structure gave way.

Nancy and Mr. March fell forward. There was no floor beyond the door. Man and girl pitched into space!

CHAPTER XXII

THE COVERED SKYLIGHT

FOR a second Nancy thought she had hurtled to the outdoors. Then she crashed onto something hard, with Mr. March beside her.

The two, their breaths knocked from them, lay still for a few moments. Then the girl roused herself.

"Are you all right?" she asked, getting up.

"Yes," panted the elderly man. "Guess we missed some steps."

The flashlight was still burning at a distance, but most of its beams were cut off by the massive wardrobe. As Nancy's eyes became accustomed to the dimness, she groped toward the doorway of the large attic to get the flashlight. Suddenly her hand touched an object which gave forth a jangle of musical notes.

"A guitar!" she exclaimed. "That may explain the mysterious sounds I heard near me when I was hunting in the other attic."

"But it doesn't explain who strummed the guitar," said Mr. March.

Nancy found the steps leading up from the old attic to the room where the skeleton hung. When she reached the place, she found Effie standing there. The maid was trembling and all the blood had drained from her face.

"I heard a crash——" she began.

"Everything is all right," said Nancy. "Mr. March and I had a little spill, but we weren't hurt."

"Thank goodness!" Effie cried. "Did you find anything?"

"Not yet. We'll let you know."

Effie went downstairs again. Nancy got the flashlight and returned to the old attic. Her first thought was to find out how the person who had bolted the door from the inner side had gained access to the room. Nothing showed up until she looked above her.

"A skylight!" she said aloud, as she played the flash on the low arched ceiling. "But it has been covered with a black cloth."

"I suppose that's how the thief we heard and never could locate got in here," said Grandfather March. "A person could step in and out of that window easily. He put the dark cloth over it to keep anyone from seeing a light in here."

Nancy was not entirely sure the elderly man was correct in his surmise about this being the entrance. There was no evidence outdoors that an intruder had any means of gaining access to the roof.

"He must be a regular steeplejack," the girl said aloud.

She and Mr. March searched for another

opening, but were unable to find one, so Nancy had to conclude Mr. March's theory must be correct.

"Now let's look for Fipp's music," said the composer's father impatiently.

The only piece of furniture in the old attic was a small antique piano-desk. Nancy inquired if Mr. March had ever seen it before.

"Yes, long ago. I'm not even sure it's the one I think it is. But I seem to recall that it was in the other attic years ago. To tell you the truth, I was away from home so much on business, that I never paid a great deal of attention to the house."

Nancy began to examine the unusual piece of furniture, feeling that if Fipp's music were hidden any place in this room, it would be there. Lightly she struck a few of the yellowed keys, and then her heart sank.

"These harplike notes are the very ones I heard the other day," she said aloud. To herself she added, "I'm afraid the intruder knew the secret of this old attic and has found all the music. One by one the songs will be published, and there won't be a scrap of evidence to bring suit against the thief! Our one clue on the staircase wall won't help us much, I'm afraid."

Grandfather March shared her feeling of discouragement as they pulled out one compartment after another of the piano-desk. They contained nothing.

"Perhaps there's a secret drawer under the keys," said Nancy, taking heart suddenly. "Those musical notes I heard may be part of the combination."

Again and again she played the tones in various positions on the piano. No hidden drawer came out.

"Didn't you say you heard tapping sounds as well?" Mr. March reminded her. "Maybe you have to tap something while you strike the notes. But what's the use of bothering if all the music is gone?"

"We don't *know* that all of it is gone. Maybe the thief was only experimenting, just as we are, to find the combination."

Cleverly Nancy endeavored to imitate the sounds exactly as she had heard them. Again she played the musical notes. Then she tapped first this part, then that of the wooden framework.

She was just about to give up, when without warning a drawer shot out just above the piano keys. Nancy and Mr. March stared in stupefaction.

"There's nothing in it!" groaned the elderly man, looking inside in profound disappointment. "The thief got here first and took it all!"

"Here's a card with writing on it," said Nancy, reaching in and taking out the message. "Maybe it gives further directions."

"Read it to me," directed Mr. March. "I can't see what it says without my glasses."

Nancy was so excited that the words tumbled from her mouth. Here, in telltale handwriting, was a splendid clue to the man who had stolen the March songs and to the person who had published them as his own original compositions! Mr. March requested that the girl repeat it.

Riggin,
  Can't you find another good song?
         L.

" 'L' for Lally, you think?" asked Mr. March excitedly.

"I'm sure of it," replied Nancy, elated at the find. "But who can Riggin be?"

At this instant Effie appeared in the doorway. "Isn't anybody going to eat supper?" she asked.

The maid's words brought the searchers back to reality.

"Why yes, Effie, we'll be right down."

"You two look awful funny. Did something happen?" Effie inquired.

"We've had a surprise, that's all," Nancy answered her. "But we didn't find what we were looking for."

Before leaving the old attic, Mr. March decided to nail up the skylight so that the intruder could not get in again. He called to Effie to bring hammer and nails.

"It's like locking the barn door after the horse has been stolen," he quoted dolefully.

"Maybe not," said Nancy, a new thought coming to her. "You know the intruder hasn't been back since we frightened him away. Whatever he wanted here he hasn't taken yet."

"True enough," agreed the elderly man. "There's still a ray of hope."

"Just where to look next puzzles me," said Nancy. "I'd like to sit down quietly and think things out."

"You'll think better after you've had something to eat," said the former soldier practically.

Nancy laughed, and admitted, now that he brought it to her attention, that she was very hungry. Effie returned with hammer and nails. The skylight was securely fastened. Then they all went below.

During supper, no mention was made of the old attic, because Susan ate with her grandfather and Nancy, and they did not want to excite the child. Conversation was light, and it was not until the little girl had gone to the kitchen after the meal was over to tell Effie something that Mr. March divulged to Nancy what he proposed to do that evening.

"I have a hunch that fellow Riggin is going to come back here tonight. Well, he'll be my prisoner before he knows what's happening to him."

"You mean you'll notify the police?"

"Indeed not. This old soldier is going to capture the thief alone!"

Nancy was aghast. "But you're not strong enough—" she started to object.

"I never felt better in my life," the elderly man declared. "And nothing would please me better than to get my hands on the fellow who stole Fipp's work!"

Nancy could not argue Mr. March out of his intentions. She offered to accompany him, but he would not let her.

"You said you wanted to think things out," he reminded her. "Maybe an idea will come to you and you'll go back to the old attic for the rest of my son's music."

"At least, let's arrange a signal," Nancy pleaded. "Couldn't you imitate some kind of an animal sound to let me know if the man should show up?"

"I can try hooting like an owl," grinned Mr. March.

"Good! I'll listen for it."

He got an overcoat and hat. Saying he would post himself near the old slave quarters, he went quietly outdoors.

Nancy put Susan to bed, then came downstairs. Effie soon finished her work and retired. The Drew girl was left alone.

A strong wind which had sprung up rattled the windows of the old mansion. Somewhere in the distance, a train whistle tooted a persistent and mournful wail.

A strange feeling of uneasiness took possession of Nancy.

CHAPTER XXIII

Sounds in the Night

For an hour Nancy sat in the dining room, thinking. She reviewed the various angles of the two strange cases in which she and her father had become involved.

"The hardest work is yet to come," she mused, "and that is going to court and proving that Mr. Dight and Mr. Lally are guilty. They've both stolen something, but how different are the two items!"

Realizing it would cost Mr. March a good bit of money to carry out his plan of prosecuting the plagiarist, Nancy could not help but wish that there were some way to locate more original music. Her thoughts turned suddenly to the piano-desk.

"Why, there may be another secret opening in it," she thought suddenly. "Why didn't I think of that before?"

Recalling a certain book on furniture that might be of use to her, Nancy got up and walked toward the former library of the old house. How loud her footsteps sounded!

Suddenly she stood still. Had she heard the hoot of an owl? The sound, however, was not repeated.

"My shoes make so much noise—" she thought as she started on.

Again she stopped. Definitely there was some noise outside. Going to the front door, the girl listened intently. She smiled, for there came a conglomeration of animal sounds; a dog barked, a cat cried, a horse neighed. But there was no hoot of an owl.

Nancy suddenly became aware of the fact that a car had just turned into the driveway. Reaching the house, the driver stopped and jumped out.

"Dad!" exclaimed Nancy, who had waited at the door to see who the newcomer might be. "Is anything wrong?"

"No, my dear," the lawyer replied. "I was passing by and thought I'd drop in to see how everything is. One of Mr. Booker's workmen got himself into trouble this evening and landed in jail. I went over to Milltown to see about his bail."

"You work at all hours, don't you?" said Nancy.

"Just as my daughter does," smiled Mr. Drew.

"I'm so glad you came, Dad. A lot of exciting things have happened since I left home."

Quickly Nancy told her father about the door hidden behind the wardrobe, of the old attic she and Mr. March had fallen into, and of the small piano-desk she suspected had held Fipp's music.

"I'm afraid all of it has been stolen," she confessed, "but there's still one little hope remaining."

"I wish I might stay here to help you in your search, but I'm due back in Milltown in twenty minutes. By the way, where's Mr. March?"

Nancy told him of the task he had taken upon himself. Her father puckered his forehead.

"The man's brave, but I believe a policeman ought to be summoned."

"I suggested that, but he just wouldn't have it that way. Why don't you stop here on your drive back?"

"The trouble is, I may be gone a couple of hours."

"Maybe Riggin won't come. As a matter of fact, I think we gave him a good scare the other night. He knows we're on guard, waiting for him."

"Who is Riggin?"

Nancy produced the note she had found in the piano-desk. Mr. Drew whistled after he had read it.

"My dear, you certainly did pick up a worthwhile piece of evidence. Perhaps that fellow Riggin realized he had lost the note and came back to get it. He may have taken all the music a long time ago."

"There's just one thing that makes me think he might not have taken all the music," said Nancy. "Grandfather March insists there were a great many songs. Only three or four of them have been published."

"So far," added Mr. Drew.

"This note says, 'Find me *another* composition.' It doesn't say 'Find me *several.*'"

"You're right," her father conceded. "Assuming the note was written recently, there is a chance of many songs still being hidden away. Well, I must go along now. Good luck to you, Nancy dear. Oh, I almost forgot. Here is a telegram for you," he added, pulling a yellow envelope from his pocket.

She read the enclosure at a glance. Horace Lally had wired to say that the "surprise" announcement in connection with the college dance had been postponed. The message ended with:

KNOW WE WILL HAVE A GRAND TIME ANYHOW. DO NOT DISAPPOINT ME.

Nancy folded the telegram and slipped it into her pocket.

"Bad news?" inquired her father.

"No, just puzzling." She told him what the telegram said. "I wonder if Horace knows his uncle is a plagiarist."

"Evidently not; and furthermore, I don't believe the boy's uncle has told him about your connection with the case," said the lawyer.

Nancy sighed. "I don't know whether that makes things better or worse. Horace doesn't write as if he knows anything about the matter."

"Well, I hope that he has had no part in it," said Mr. Drew. "That sort of thing is nasty business to be mixed up in. Now I must be going, Nancy," he concluded.

After her father had left, Nancy continued to mull over the unfortunate affair. She did not like Horace, yet she had never thought of him as being connected with any dishonest dealings.

"I just can't believe such a thing," the girl told herself. "However, he did say the surprise announcement concerned a friend of mine. In the light of what has happened, that could mean nobody but himself."

A new idea came to Nancy. Maybe the thief named Riggin had sold the stolen songs to various people, and they in turn had brought them out under assumed names. Could it be possible that Horace Lally was Harry Hall?

"One thing is certain," the girl decided. "The farther I stay away from him, the better!"

Nancy turned to the book on old furniture, and began thumbing through its pages. Chairs, tables, beds—all were described in detail. Then on the very last page a piano-desk was pictured. Eagerly the girl detective read a description of it.

" '—often had secret trays—the one in the illustration has two. On the right side of the upper part of the desk is a secret spring——' "

Nancy read no more. Excited, she jumped up and started for the attic. Mr. March had taken the flashlight with him, so the girl obtained a candle. Reaching the third floor, she proceeded at once to the old attic.

At the very moment when she set down her light on a corner of the piano-desk, a harrowing scene was taking place below in the garden near the former slave quarters. Grandfather March, weary and heavy-eyed from his long vigil, had decided he would have to walk around a bit to keep from going to sleep. Just as he emerged from the shadows, a stealthy figure, crossing the lawn, saw the elderly man and guessed that he was on watch.

"I'll change my course and fool him!" the sneaking intruder decided.

Accordingly he made a wide detour and approached his enemy from the front of the old mansion. As Mr. March, unsuspecting, turned to face the rear of the house, the skulking figure hurried forward noiselessly.

Raising his arm, he brought down his huge fist on top of the elderly gentleman's head. As Grandfather March reeled sideways, a faint groan escaping from his lips, his attacker followed the first blow with a second one on the jaw.

Completely knocked out, the former soldier fell to the ground. Gloating in satisfaction, the mysterious stranger ran toward the house.

CHAPTER XXIV

The Trap

A CLOCK chimed the witching hour of midnight.

"Twelve o'clock, and all's well, I hope," Nancy said, as she started her new investigation of the piano-desk.

The utter stillness and the close atmosphere of the old attic had a depressing effect upon her. She began to breathe more quickly as first one sound, then another came to her ears.

"They seem so far away," she thought. "I wonder if I could hear Mr. March if he should call."

For a long moment Nancy stood still, hesitating to go on with her work. Maybe she ought to run downstairs to be near the elderly man if he should need her.

"I'll hurry," she decided. "It won't take a minute to find that secret tray."

Following the directions in the book, Nancy pressed the side of the old piece of furniture. No drawer came out.

"Maybe this piano-desk isn't like the one in the picture," she thought in disappointment.

Nevertheless she tried again, switching from the right to the left-hand side. Suddenly her candle began to flicker wildly.

In panic Nancy looked in the direction of the doorway. No one was there. She glanced toward the skylight. It was tightly closed.

"What made that current of air?" she asked. The candle stopped flickering. Quickly the girl went on with her task. At last her efforts were rewarded.

Slowly, and with strained stops and starts, a shallow tray moved out from the upper left side of the old piano-desk. It was filled with papers.

Before Nancy could take out any of them, the tray began to recede. Again the candle flickered and nearly went out. Suddenly the drawer clicked shut as if some invisible force had drawn it back. Nancy's pulses beat wildly, but she forced herself to be calm.

"Some mechanism must have caused the drawer to shut," she reasoned. "No doubt there's a catch to hold it open!"

With frantic haste she groped again for the secret spring. Her fingers encountered it, and the drawer slowly opened. Nancy felt underneath it and located a tiny lever which she moved. The tray did not close this time.

Within lay several scrolls and folded papers. Nancy scanned them hastily. As she had hoped, they were all musical compositions. The name Philip March, Jr. was signed in a bold scrawl at the top of each song!

"These have never been published!" she thought elatedly. "That thief didn't find them!"

Her imagination ran riot as she hummed one lovely air after another and realized what hits they would make. She could picture the shabby old mansion restored to its former grandeur. Mr. March, nattily attired, would be welcoming musicians to his home to receive their congratulations. Little Susan would be getting a fine education——

Nancy was so absorbed in her thoughts that she failed to notice a figure watching her intently from behind. A trapdoor in the ceiling of the old slave quarters had opened. Noiselessly, a man had raised himself through the space. Now he was smiling evilly.

"So she found it for me!" he gloated.

With catlike tread he approached the girl, coming nearer—nearer——

Nancy, unaware that her every move was being watched, closed the drawer. She gathered together all the manuscripts and prepared to leave the old attic. As she started to pick up the candle, it flickered violently. At the same instant, she became aware of a giant shadow on the floor. Someone was behind her!

Nancy froze to the spot. The stealthy intruder confronted her. Before she could scream, he grabbed her and put his hand over her mouth.

"Bushy Trott!" she gurgled behind his fat fingers.

"Mr. Riggin Trott, if you please!" he corrected her with a sneer. "I see you remember me. Well, I remember *you*. Tried to spy on me at the Dight factory, didn't you? Well, that didn't get you anywhere!"

Nancy fought to escape from the man, but his clutch was like an iron vice. He whipped out a handkerchief and stuffed it into Nancy's mouth. Deftly he produced two pieces of rope from his pocket.

"Always carry these for emergencies," he announced with a low chuckle.

Nancy kicked at his shins, and he winced with pain.

"Goin' to fight, eh? I'll soon fix those stubborn feet of yours," he sneered, his eyes burning angrily.

Having tied Nancy's hands behind her, Trott now pushed the girl down and bound her ankles together. She fought desperately, and at one point almost got away from him. His great bulk and bulging muscles were overpowering, however. When he had her completely at his mercy, he stood looking down at her, grinning evilly.

"Many thanks for solving a baffling mystery!" he said. "For a long while I've been trying to learn where the rest of the March music was hidden. Now I'll relieve you of your precious bundle."

He picked up the manuscripts, which had fallen to the floor in the scuffle, and put them under one arm. Then he reached into a pocket.

"I'm sorry to leave you like this," he said

sardonically, "but I trust that this little creature will fix you so that you'll remember nothing of this episode."

Nancy, squirming and twisting, did not understand what the man meant. He removed a bottle from his pocket.

"You wonder what this is, my pretty?" he jested cruelly. "A tarantula spider, my dear. Oh, you shudder? Then you know what it will do to you."

Never before in all her life had Nancy been in a worse trap. Not only was she utterly helpless to defend herself, but she realized that there was no one to rescue her before the poison of the tarantula might have a deadly effect upon her.

Bushy Trott's eyes gleamed like a maniac's as he laid the spider on a corner of the piano-desk. At once it started to crawl toward the floor.

"*Maybe* you won't die right away," the evil fellow whispered hoarsely. "Sometimes the poison only gives you that strange disease called tarantism. Ever hear of it? You lose your memory, and then your mind compels you to dance until you fall unconscious!"

During the scuffle the note addressed to Riggin, which Nancy had found in the tray of the piano-desk, had fallen from her pocket. The man reached down and scooped it up.

"Where'd you get this?" he demanded, but he did not remove the gag from the girl's mouth so that she could tell him. "It doesn't matter, now that I've got it back. I should a' burned it up."

The tarantula had reached the floor now. Nancy rolled herself sideways to get out of its path.

Her eyes focused for a second on the steps leading to the big attic. If only she could pull herself up into that other room, she might yet escape.

She figured that Trott planned to leave soon. She wished that he would go right away! In a moment she understood why he was in no hurry.

"Don't expect any help from the old man," the bushy-haired fellow said with a look of satisfaction. "He's sound asleep in the garden, and he won't wake up for a long, long time. I saw to that!"

He chuckled, pleased with his accomplishment. Nancy's heart nearly stopped beating. What had he done to Mr. March?

"Now just to be sure nobody else comes here," Trott continued, "I'll lock this door!"

To Nancy's complete alarm, he moved to the opening through which she had hoped to escape. He swung the battered door shut. In a moment he nailed into place again the long, wooden bar which she and Mr. March had broken down.

Thoroughly enjoying himself, Bushy Trott looked around. Seeing the spider, he scooped it up in the bottle and shook it, "just to liven the thing up a bit," he said. Once more the man held it above the piano-desk. The tarantula crawled out and dropped onto the yellowed keys of the instrument.

"I always carry one of these or else a black widow with me in case of need," Trott explained. "Well, good night, young lady!" he grinned at Nancy, "and good-by."

To her horror he picked up the candle and retreated to the trapdoor. Nancy, lying on the floor, struggled desperately to free herself.

"You only waste your strength, my pretty," Trott taunted her. "You cannot escape. The tarantula may not come quickly, but he will find you at last."

The man flashed his light on the piano. Nancy saw the tarantula climbing slowly down the leg of the instrument, not a dozen feet away from her.

"Sweet dreams, my dear!" whispered Trott, blowing out the candle.

He took a flashlight from his pocket, turned it on, then lowered himself through the opening in the floor.

Nancy wondered whether he closed the trapdoor, for she could hear no sound except his own footsteps as he went down the rickety stairs of the slave quarters.

The old attic was in complete blackness. Nancy knew the tarantula was coming closer to her, but she had no idea which way to roll to avoid its deadly bite.

CHAPTER XXV

The Plotter Nabbed

Nancy lay very still. She felt that the tarantula must be close to her. At any moment the poisonous spider might strike.

Many thoughts raced through her mind. Her wonderful father—she shuddered to contemplate his feelings if anything should happen to her—and faithful Hannah Gruen, who had reared her with the affection of a mother. Bess, George, Ned——

Suddenly Nancy's anger at the perpetrator of this vile deed took possession of her. No one but she herself could testify that he was the thief of Fipp March's music, and that he carried deadly black widows and tarantulas with him to use on any who might stand in his way. No telling how many persons had been his victims!

"How can I get out of here?" Nancy asked herself over and over again. "That terrible man must not be allowed at large. I must do something."

She could not scream, nor could she loosen her bonds. However, she found she was able to raise both feet and thump them hard on the floor. Would the sounds carry to Effie's room?

And if they did, would the timid maid break down the door and venture into the old attic?

Nancy rolled herself across the floor until she came to the steps. Then she pounded again with all her might. After waiting several minutes and getting no response, she gave up hope of rescue from this direction.

Suddenly the girl thought of the trapdoor. Maybe it was still open. Without figuring out just how she might escape by this means, she cautiously hitched herself toward the spot, hoping not to meet the tarantula on the way. Though she covered every inch of the surrounding space, Nancy failed to find any opening.

"Bushy Trott must have closed it," she decided. "And in this darkness I'd have no idea how to find out the way it works."

Her last means of escape was gone! In the past Nancy had faced many situations which called for high courage. Waiting in the darkness now was the most trying ordeal of her life.

In imagination, the girl suddenly heard her name called. It seemed faint and far away. Then somewhere hurrying footsteps sounded.

"Nancy! Nancy!" a voice called out.

The cries could not be real! Yet they sounded as if they were! Nancy strained to hear better. Suddenly, daring to hope, she thumped again on the attic floor.

"Nancy! Where are you?" shouted somebody.

She had not imagined it. Now she could hear

jumbled voices in the big attic. Again her name was called.

The girl thumped with all her strength. The next instant a body crashed against the door, and it burst open. A flashlight shone in Nancy's eyes.

"Thank goodness, you're alive!" were the words the girl heard. The speaker was Ned Nickerson!

Bess, George, and Effie crowded into the room after him. But the youth took complete charge of the situation.

Springing forward, he jerked the gag from Nancy's mouth. Then he cut her fetters with his pocketknife and tenderly helped her to her feet. The supporting arm he slipped about her waist trembled.

"Nancy, if anything had happened to you—" he mumbled. "Why, I can't even bear to think of it."

Nancy gazed at Ned in wonder. For a young man who had not been in touch with her for some time, and had invited another girl to the Emerson dance, he certainly was not acting in character.

"Who did this to you?" he demanded gruffly.

"Bushy Trott. Oh, Ned——"

Nancy felt light-headed. As she sagged sideways, the boy picked her up. How good his strong arms felt!

"Oh, Nancy, you're ill! That brute has injured you!"

Before she could tell him she would be all right in a minute, Effie let out a horrible screech. Her eyes bulging, she pointed to the floor. They all looked. The horrible tarantula was not two feet away.

Still holding Nancy, Ned crushed the spider with his foot. Effie's scream had brought the Drew girl out of her momentary feeling of faintness. She released herself from Ned's arms.

"Have you seen Grandfather March, any of you?" she asked quickly.

The others gazed at her, perplexed.

"Ain't he in bed?" asked Effie.

In a few words Nancy told them Bushy Trott's sinister words. Like a shot George was through the door of the old attic and on her way to the garden. Bess and Effie followed quickly.

Nancy started after them, but Ned held her back. He gazed at the girl so intently that she blushed to the roots of her hair.

"Are you telling me the truth?" he begged. "Are you really all right?"

"Yes, Ned, really," she smiled at him. "I was pretty scared for a while, I admit, but when you came—Ned, maybe you don't know it, but you saved my life! I shall always be thankful to you."

"It would have been my very great loss if I hadn't," he said fervently, and again she flushed crimson.

He released her hand, and together they went

downstairs quickly. Effie and the girls were searching outdoors for Mr. March.

"By the slave quarters," called Nancy.

She led the way as Ned held the flashlight. Under a lilac bush they found the crumpled form of Susan's grandfather. Effie let out a frightened moan.

"Is he—is he——"

Ned pulled the still figure from beneath the bush. Nancy felt the elderly man's pulse.

"He's alive," she said. "But the shock may prove to be too much for him."

They carried him into the house. Under their kindly ministrations, he quickly regained consciousness. Nancy had warned the others not to tell him what had happened in the attic. Presently he dozed off into a normal slumber.

"I have to go to River Heights right away," said Nancy. "Effie, I can't explain now, but you'll be all right here alone. That shadowy figure will never come back."

"Thank goodness!" said the maid. "That's all right, Miss Nancy. You and your friends go right along, and I'll take good care o' Mr. March."

"Where are you going?" asked George.

"To Mr. Dight."

"Then you know——"

"I know he has the address of Bushy Trott!"

"What!"

Explanations were in order on both sides. Nancy suggested they tell their stories while riding along. When they went outside, the young people saw a car turn into Pleasant Hedges. The driver proved to be Mr. Drew.

"What luck!" cried Nancy. "Oh, Dad," she said hurriedly, as he stopped, "can you go to Mr. Dight's house with us right away?"

"Sure can," he replied. "But what's up?"

"It was Bushy Trott who was stealing Fipp March's music! And he got away with all the rest of it tonight! We'll get his address from Mr. Dight and then notify the police!"

"Hop in, everybody!" called out Carson Drew.

Bess and George climbed in front beside the lawyer, leaving Nancy and Ned to ride in the back seat alone. She was amused at her chums' pointed action, but Ned was delighted.

Nancy gave her father and her friends the story of her evening's adventure in detail. At Nancy's recital of her experience of being tied up in the dark with a tarantula, Mr. Drew nearly went off the road.

"You shouldn't take such chances," he scolded his daughter.

"Anyway, it's fortunate that my friends rescued me," replied Nancy cheerfully.

"It was just luck we did," Ned explained. "Tonight when I came back to River Heights, I bumped into Bess and George. When I found out you weren't away with your father, I knew something was wrong. Even though it was late, we decided to come out here to square matters with you."

"I don't understand."

"I believe Diane Dight pulled a fast one on both of us. You haven't received a telegram from me lately, have you, Nancy?"

"Why no, Ned," was the girl's reply.

"Then that practically proves it!"

"Proves what?"

"That Diane tricked us. You see, I sent a wire inviting you to the Emerson dance. The reply I received said you couldn't come because you were going on a trip with your father."

"What!"

"This is the way Bess and I figure it," said George. "Apparently Diane learned about the dance from her cousin Horace. She wanted to go with Ned, so she intercepted the telegram meant for you, Nancy."

"But how could she know about it?"

"She didn't. She hoped Ned would send one, and waited to stop the messenger boy before he could deliver it to you. It was her only chance, and she was lucky," George explained in disgust.

"I should have telephoned afterward," declared Ned.

"How did you happen to invite Diane?" asked Bess.

"She came to Emerson and tried to make it seem casual when we met. She got there not long after the telegram came. Practically invited herself to go to the dance with me. But she's not going!" he added firmly. "*You* are, Nancy."

"She'd never forgive you, Ned," said the girl beside him. "Maybe she didn't send the telegram at all."

"Whether she did or didn't, you had the first invitation. I'll get the telegraph company to prove it."

Nancy laughed. Then she said in a low voice, "One day I called on Diane and saw the envelope of a letter you had written her. I admit I had a shock, because——"

"Yes?"

"Because she doesn't seem like the kind of girl you would be writing letters to."

"Oh!" Ned had hoped Nancy was going to say something different. "Diane had written to ask what kind of clothes to bring," he explained.

"Diane was so proud of the fact that Ned was taking her that she bragged about it to Horace. That's why Horace asked you, Nancy," said George.

Mr. Drew had reached River Heights. Bess thought that she and George ought to go home, so the girls were dropped at their respective houses.

"You can't get rid of me, though," laughed Ned. "I'm not going to let this night pass without finding out if Diane sent that telegram!"

"Glad to have you anyway," said Mr. Drew. "We may need a strong man before the night's over!"

It was nearing two o'clock when the party

drove up to the darkened Dight home. Mr. Drew pounded and pounded on the front door. Finally the manufacturer came to let them in.

"What's the meaning of this?" he demanded.

The lawyer did not waste words. He stated that he wanted to prefer charges against Riggin Trott and demanded the man's address.

"I don't even know the follow," Mr. Dight blustered. "What do you mean by coming here at this time of the morning?"

"Maybe you know him as Bushy Trott. We have proof that he stole a chemical silk-making process from his former employer, Mr. Booker," snapped the lawyer. "You are using that same formula in your own plant."

"Bosh!"

"There is no side-stepping it," declared Mr. Drew coldly. "My daughter obtained samples of fluid from your laboratory. Tests prove them to have the same content as the Booker mixtures."

Nancy spoke up. "Your employee Trott to-night tried to kill me by tying me up and turning a tarantula loose."

The information seemed to stun Mr. Dight.

"I knew nothing of a tarantula," he insisted in a frightened voice. "We have poisonous spiders at our plant but no tarantulas."

"There are other charges against the man also. Will you give me his address, or——"

Mr. Dight was shaking.

"Yes, I will. I assure you I did not know

ingly use the Booker silk-making process. Nor did I suspect that Trott was trying to make trouble for your daughter.''

Mr. Dight went quickly to a desk. As he wrote down Trott's home address on a sheet of paper, the callers heard footsteps on the stairway.

Nancy looked up and saw Diane on the first landing. The girl came slowly down to the hall, her glance roving from Ned to the others.

"Oh, Father," she whined, "I didn't mean any harm by sending the telegram. Please don't punish me."

"Telegram?" questioned her father. "What are you talking about?"

Belatedly the girl realized that Nancy and Ned had not come to the house to report her behavior. She then tried to retreat, but her father would not permit her to go until he had heard her entire story. Not only did he reprimand his daughter severely, but he told her she would get no allowance for a long time to come.

"You're mean!" Diane stormed childishly as she ran from the room. "I didn't intend any harm, and it's cruel to treat me like this!"

Mr. Dight not only apologized to Nancy for his daughter's behavior, but for his own as well.

"To tell you the truth, I thought for a time you were trying to steal our plant formulas," he explained. "We purchased the new silk-making process from Trott at great cost recently. I've kept that part of the factory a secret, because

I was afraid all the workmen in the place might leave if they knew there were poisonous spiders around.''

"The secret you guard so carefully already belongs to my client, Mr. Booker," replied Carson Drew. "The only difference is that your man uses poisonous spiders. From what happened tonight, I judge he has a mania for the deadly things."

"You mean to say Bushy Trott sold me a process which he neither owned nor controlled?"

"Exactly."

"Then I've been tricked!" shouted the factory owner. "I'll telephone the police immediately and have the man arrested."

Within ten minutes a patrol car was speeding to the Trott home. Mr. Drew, Nancy, and Ned followed in the lawyer's automobile. They arrived in time to see the bushy-haired crook led from the house by two policemen. He turned deathly white when he saw the Drew girl.

"You?" he cried unbelievingly.

"Is this the fellow you want?" one of the officers asked Nancy, seeking a positive identification.

"Yes," she replied. "I believe his right name is Riggin Trott."

Nancy and her father were permitted to question the man at Headquarters. Police supplied the information that he was an ex-convict, though unquestionably a clever chemist. It came out that after a short prison career he had worked as a servant for Ben Lally.

"Ben Lally!" cried Nancy. "Well, that explains a number of things! You sold the music to him?"

Trott nodded. The girl got several damaging admissions from the man. Some were facts already suspected by her—that he had loaded the old rifle, strummed the guitar, and smoked in the old attic. Other items were entirely new.

Not only had the man stolen the Booker silk-making formula, but for a long time he had been trying to rob Grandfather March of Fipp's songs. Having found three good ones, he longed for more.

Trott had served three years in the State Penitentiary on a charge of robbery. While thus confined, he had become very proficient at bench work. Being already well versed in chemistry, it was easy for him to copy the Booker method and sell it to a competitor.

Following his release from prison, he had served Ben Lally as a personal servant and valet. Times were difficult, and Lally, always struggling to produce a song which would sell, was hard pressed financially.

At this point Trott slyly suggested to his employer that he knew where saleable songs might be obtained. Desperate for funds, Lally had listened to him with interest.

As it developed, Trott several years before had planned to rob the March homestead. While getting the lay of the land there one day, he had overheard Fipp tell his wife he was going to put the music away until he should come back to his home again. Trott had seen him go to the attic with it.

A few years later, Trott had returned. One day when the family was away, he came to explore the attic. He had found the crude door covered by the heavy wardrobe and had investigated the second room. He had found one song which had been left on the piano-desk. This he had sold to Lally, who had written him asking for more.

"I thought that skeleton was a good idea," said Trott, "so I put it back in place. Then I made myself a trapdoor up to the old attic. Clever, wasn't it? You didn't find it," he gloated.

Many a night Trott had secretly entered the March house by this means. His shadow had terrified Effie, and his footsteps had echoed weirdly through the old mansion. In vain the man had searched for the mass of missing music. Once the drawer above the keys had opened and two songs had been revealed. Here Trott had dropped the telltale note.

The few pieces he was able to turn over to Ben Lally, who had them published under the names of Ben Banks and Harry Hall, quickly made an impression upon the public. The publisher's eager plea for more compositions made Bushy determined to find all Fipp's creations.

Trott was convinced that the hidden music must be somewhere in or about the piano-desk.

As his searching activities went on, he became alarmed, thinking that he might be caught, because Nancy and her friends came with increasing frequency to the attic.

Cunningly Trott decided to frighten everyone away. He bored a hole through the secret door and the back of the wardrobe. Then he released a deadly black widow spider, which later crawled through the tiny opening to bite Effie.

As for Ben Lally, the success of the first stolen songs overcame his scruples. He urged Trott to find other compositions for him. It was not until the second song had been put on the market that the publisher learned his client was not the composer. There had been words and threats on both sides, but finally Mr. Jenner, already making money on the musical hits, had decided that probably no one ever would learn the truth, so he had promised to keep the matter a secret.

Ben Lally, now in Trott's clutches, aided the man in various crimes. He sent him to his gullible brother-in-law Dight, and planned to profit handsomely from the sale of the stolen silk-making process. Lally's one redeeming quality was an honest interest and affection for his orphaned nephew, Horace.

"At least, I'm glad Horace had no part in the disgraceful affair," Nancy commented to Bess and George a couple of days later. "How ashamed he must feel of his uncle."

"What was to have been his part in the surprise announcement at the dance?" George inquired.

"He leads the orchestra, as you know," Nancy replied. "It seems his uncle suggested Horace play one of his songs, and the boy had worked out a clever orchestral arrangement for it."

"It's too bad Horace is mixed up in it," sighed Bess. "I understand he's leaving town. For that matter, so are the Dights."

"Oh, I hadn't heard about it."

"Yes, Mr. and Mrs. Dight and Diane will spend several months on the West Coast, according to the River Heights *Gazette*. They're taking Horace with them."

"Then I shan't have to worry about meeting him at Emerson," Nancy said in relief. "Would you like to see what I'm going to wear?" she asked, her eyes sparkling.

The three girls went upstairs. From her closet Nancy brought out a pale yellow evening dress, soft and beautiful in texture.

"Oh!" cried Bess, "I never saw anything lovelier. Where did you get it?"

"A Mr. Booker sent it to me. He's a client of Dad's." Nancy wished she might tell them more, but she had promised the manufacturer she would not divulge his secret.

"I'll bet you helped your Dad on a case," said George wisely, "and that's your reward. I wish my father knew somebody who would give me a gorgeous dress like that!"

Nancy laughed, and asked what other local news her friends had read in the *Gazette*.

"I haven't had time to look at the papers lately," she confessed.

"The best item hasn't been printed yet," Bess replied. "But it will be after the dance tomorrow night."

"What's that?"

Her friend's eyes twinkled.

"The society page will carry a paragraph which will read: 'Miss Nancy Drew, escorted by Ned Nickerson, was unquestionably the most popular young lady at the ball.' "

"I'll let someone else carry off the social honors," Nancy replied, smiling. "I'll stick to mystery."

True to her word, the girl soon found an opportunity to solve another perplexing case, "The Clue in the Crumbling Wall."

"You've made two firm friends," said Mr. Drew to his daughter one day. "I just stopped in to call on Mr. March and Susan. The wonderful things they had to say about you! And Mr. March is feeling very well again."

"I'm glad to have helped them," smiled Nancy modestly. "And it was exciting prowling around their third floor."

"Nevertheless, it took courage," replied her father. "If you hadn't had it, you never would have discovered the secret of the old attic."

THE END